Neon Hemlock Press
www.neonhemlock.com
@neonhemlock

© 2025 Caitlin Starling

The Oblivion Bride
Caitlin Starling

Cover Illustration by Ocean Salazar
Cover Design and Interior Layout by dave ring
Edited by dave ring

Print ISBN-13: 978-1-952086-93-9
Ebook ISBN-13: 978-1-966503-01-9

Caitlin Starling
THE OBLIVION BRIDE
Neon Hemlock Press

THE OBLIVION BRIDE

BY CAITLIN STARLING

For Callista

Stars veil their beauty soon
Beside the glorious moon,
When her full silver light
Doth make the whole earth bright.
—*Sappho*

ONE

LORELEI STEDDART, HEIR to the House of Pharyn, sits at the conference table where she will negotiate her marriage. In front of her is a leather folder filled with notes, assumptions, expectations. There are no photos. No profiles. She should be afraid for her future, but it's hard to focus; even her nerves can't pierce through the dull wrap of grief that has swaddled her tight for the past six months.

She's been allowed to wear her mourning white, even while they've bleached her hair back to its natural blonde and stuffed her into a sharply tailored, pinched-waist dress with a spangled brooch at her right hip. The hair, the dress, the necklace that glitters at her throat: all fit her, and yet do not fit her. Six months ago, she would never have worn anything so rich.

Six months ago, she wouldn't have been sold off into marriage.

Her uncle sits down next to her, either satisfied with his defensive prowling about the glass-walled room they wait in, or finally giving in to boredom. He, at least, looks natural inside a high government building, wearing his bespoke suit. *He* would have been here six months ago. But sitting where Lorelei is now would have been his eldest daughter, Gwyndofir, and she would have had some say in the match.

Instead, her bones were burned to ash five weeks ago. The white of her uncle's suit is blinding. The shadows beneath his eyes are all the darker for it.

"Chin up," he says. "They will be here soon. They know how it would look to keep us waiting. We are not here to beg."

The words make her skin crawl, and she has to bear down on herself with all her might to keep from standing up, from fleeing the room. She wants to be in her old apartment. She wants to be by her mother's memorial stone. She wants to be out past the city walls, where the land shifts with every step, and give herself over to the wild magic beyond civilization.

She does not want to be here, waiting to be bargained off in exchange for the future of her uncle's House.

Motion out in the hallway catches her eye, a coterie of bustling suits. Aides, lawyers, advisors, all flocking around the Prince of Volun. She rises to her feet just a few milliseconds after her uncle does, but she knows she will be rebuked for it later. She never learned all the proper forms of address, the tiny gradations of the highest echelons of polite society.

Rifting take her, she was working in an office six months ago. She didn't even have a trust fund, let alone…

All this.

All this, because her family is dying.

Is dead.

She watches the mob approach, and fights to slow her breathing, tries to feel something beyond the stabbing grief and the wretched anger that is burning a hole in her heart. Even panic would be welcome, would seem appropriate.

And then the crowd in the hallway parts, as if a spell has created a column of floor, two feet wide, where none was before. Not even the prince was given so much space. The backs of Lorelei's knees bump against her seat as she instinctively tries to retreat. Down the center of that column of floor walks a woman nearly six feet in height. Her dark hair is shot through with grey, her eyes framed with an elaborate metal limiter that stretches from cheek and brow to temple and jaw. Beneath the woven metal, Lorelei can make out rippled, glowing scars, pulsing a deep indigo. It's as if the limiter is keeping her skull together, not just keeping her from blowing them all up.

The woman walks with studied confidence, pinstriped suit moving with her, never pulling awkwardly. She wears a decorative cape, held in place at her right shoulder with an elaborate pin that proclaims her rank.

She doesn't need to wear it. Everybody knows that face. Everybody knows that cold, removed stare. Lorelei has seen it on the news a thousand times.

"War Alchemist Corisande," she whispers.

Her uncle sucks in a tight breath behind her.

The prince's aide opens the door, and the ruler of Volun steps in, followed by what looks like two lawyers— and the war alchemist. The rest of the mob peels off and goes their separate directions, orders issued.

"Well, Lord Steddart," the prince says, extending a hand across the table. "It is good to see you on a happy occasion this time around."

Instead of at a funeral, he means.

"It is indeed," her uncle replies, bending down to kiss the prince's ring. His lips do not touch the stone, and his hand doesn't touch the prince's. Proper form, or acknowledgment of potential contagion? He straightens. "May I introduce Lorelei, my half-sister's daughter?"

Six months ago, that *half* would have been important. It had meant she was the last in line for inheritance. Now it means nothing at all; whatever is striking down her family doesn't care about parentage or marriages. It only cares about the blood.

The numb spiral of her thoughts revolts in another sudden burst of pain, but Lorelei forces herself to keep moving, imitating her uncle's gesture.

"She does have your father's countenance," the prince says. He regards her, canting his head to one side. Lorelei avoids his gaze. "Well, Miss Steddart. What is your mind about this marriage?"

Heart pounding in her ears, she says, "That I'm very lucky to have such a matchmaker."

Her voice cracks.

The rehearsed line amuses the prince, who laughs and pulls out his chair. He sits, and so do the lawyers, and her uncle, and Lorelei. Only the war alchemist remains standing.

Her uncle hazards a glance towards her. "And you, War Alchemist? Will you be assisting in finding the match?"

Lorelei glances up at her, sees the older woman's mouth tense. But it is the prince who speaks.

"War Alchemist Corisande is here to *be* the match."

Lorelei's shy glance becomes a terrified, disbelieving stare. Corisande gazes back, coolly.

"Miss Steddart, I am pleased to introduce you to your wife. Nephele?"

The woman inclines her head. "Miss Steddart," she says.

Lorelei can't speak, not even when her uncle taps her shoe with his below the table.

"We are honored," he says for her. "Though I have to admit to some…curiosity."

Some confusion. As heir to the house of Pharyn, Lorelei should be matched with a similar scion, or at least a wealthy businessperson. Nephele Corisande is high-ranked and quite well-off, but she brings no land, no enduring status, no lineage—nothing but her own reputation to the match.

A reputation as an ice-cold soldier, elegant in her brutality on the battlefield, brilliant in her innovations of martial spellwork.

Lorelei can't look away from her, not even when Corisande's jaw tightens in annoyance, not even when the other woman turns her gaze to the far wall, looking ahead blankly as she falls into parade rest.

"I understand," the prince says, "that initial tests have shown no cohesive factor between all the deaths in your line. Is that correct?"

Her uncle fidgets in his seat. He hides it well by reaching for his glass of water, but Lorelei can feel her own pained response to the topic echoing back from him.

"That is correct," her uncle says. "Most have been illnesses, and a few have been of the same type, but taken as a whole, there has been no consistency."

The doctors are at a loss. Her mother is dead, and even now has no diagnosis. Lorelei fists the fabric of her skirt between her fingers, weathering a storm of anger and grief and agony.

"It's probably magical in origin," Corisande says.

Her voice cuts through the fog.

"I assure you," Lorelei's uncle says, "we're all properly warded."

"Then shall we blame divine judgment?" Corisande asks, voice level, no trace of cruelty in her mockery. "Wards can only go so far, and even the best only defend against whatever they were built to withstand. I am here to investigate."

"Do we have to be married for that?"

Everybody turns to Lorelei then, but she barely notices. She is fixated on Corisande. The anger leaps up in her gullet again, followed by desperation, and then, worst of all, hope. Hope that Corisande can help.

"Strictly speaking, no," the prince says. "However, the marriage would solve a host of other issues. And what the war alchemist lacks in an inherited title, she makes up for with circumspection and her own status as—"

"Nobody else would agree to it, would they?" Lorelei asks.

Her uncle grabs her wrist below the table, pressing firmly.

She knows what he wants, but she doesn't want to behave. She wants to scream. She wants to tear the whole room apart. She wants…

So much. And only this: that the nightmare be over, that it could have never begun at all.

The prince's lips quirk in a wry, surprised smile. "You're very perceptive."

"Your Highness, I apologize for my niece's bluntness. I assure you—"

"Spare me." The prince leans across the table toward her, splaying one ringed hand on the wood. "You're correct, Miss Steddart. Nobody else is prepared to take on the risk, however nebulous, that attachment to your family appears to confer. And while we could postpone your marriage during General Corisande's investigations, and try again once you are hopefully cleared of all threat, should something unfortunate befall you in the meantime, somebody must be in a position to handle the assets of the House of Pharyn." He lifts one shoulder in an elegant shrug, and adds, almost as an afterthought, "Your uncle also made very clear to me that the issue of an heir was to be a top priority in the match."

Her cheeks heat. Her throat goes dry. "And the general…"

"Agrees to legitimize any children you bear, by whatever means."

Lorelei looks up at the War Alchemist, and is met with an impassive gaze. No flicker of embarrassment or interest as the prince sits back, spreading his hands in offering.

"You may conduct yourself in whatever way the House of Pharyn approves of; there will be no contractual obligations in the arrangement except that you do not divorce, and that you assist General Corisande in her investigations."

"This is very unorthodox," her uncle begins, and she thinks he's about to disagree, thinks he's about to argue that the search should be widened. Instead, he says, "However, we appreciate your dedication to finding a solution to our peculiar needs. We accept."

TWO●

THE NEXT MORNING, Lorelei's uncle takes her to a
fertility clinic.

He doesn't ask. She doesn't protest. She's
considered having children before, and come down on the
generally-in-favor side, but never put any further thought
into it. Now there's no point. She must have children.
She must carry on the line. Not just one child, then, but
many, and so she'd better get started.

Nephele Corisande meets them in the waiting
room. She hasn't dressed down for the occasion. Suit,
cape, gleaming power limiter plastered to her temples
and cheekbones, not a hair out of place. Lorelei feels
embarrassed; she's still in all white, still in cashmere, but
it's a simple wrap sweater and skirt, all the easier to drop
for the reproductive specialist.

So this is how it's going to be: her uncle making plans with
her future wife, even before the formality of the engagement
ceremony, and Lorelei tugged along where she needs to go.

Best get used to being an empty vessel, dear; you'll be filled soon enough.

The thought is as uncharitable as it is accurate, and she fixes her eyes on one of the tasteful paintings on the waiting room wall. No posters for public health initiatives here. No other patients waiting, either. Just fine furniture, delicate wallpaper, gentle lighting. Only the best for the last chance pony. No room for her to court those *other methods* of getting knocked up they'd alluded to at the conference table. There's no time for her to take a lover. No time for anything but... this.

"Lorelei," her uncle says, and she realizes she's missed out on some bit of conversation.

The war alchemist is looking at her, plainly unimpressed.

"My apologies," Lorelei stammers, averting her gaze. "What was that?"

"War Alchemist Corisande asked if you'd prefer a boy or a girl."

There is a sudden ringing in her ears, the question too intimate, too unreal to handle. She's melting and freezing and decomposing all at once. "Either," she says, then, inelegantly, "both?"

She's saved from further humiliation by a nurse coming to fetch them.

The lighting in the exam room is brighter, more clinical, but the room is heated and arranged for comfort. The exam table doesn't face the door or the chairs. She won't be able to see her uncle or Corisande while the doctor examines her, but then, they won't be able to see her, either.

The nurse takes her vitals from an invitingly cushioned chair. Her uncle keeps up a calm patter: the weather, local restaurants, and yes, of course, they'd like the full panel right off the bat. Lorelei rolls up her sleeve for the nurse to draw her blood.

The nurse leaves. Corisande follows. Her uncle lingers long enough to frown at her.

"Behave, Lorelei. I know this is uncomfortable, but we must cooperate."

She nearly opens her mouth to argue. *I am cooperating! I'm here!* But cooperation isn't just acquiescence, she's learning, it's doing it with a smile, it's doing it without honesty. Honesty, reality, no longer matters.

It's just duty.

Alone, she peels off her skirt. Her hands are shaking. Her cheeks are hot, her face swollen with the force of all the anger and humiliation burning inside of her, and she has to bite her painted lip not to cry. She folds the skirt neatly, tucks her underwear beneath it on the seat. Then she climbs up on the table, lined with soft fabric instead of the crinkly paper she's used to, and covers her lap with the blanket she's been given. This, too, is actually large enough to cover, pleasant to touch.

She wonders if anybody who has access to these luxuries is in a position to enjoy them, or if it's always like this.

Lorelei prepares herself for an interminable wait, but the knock comes not even a minute later.

She must have mumbled some permission, though it's lost to the buzzing inside her skull. Footsteps behind her, her uncle preceding the doctor, preceding Corisande. And then the exam, which she lies back and does her best to ignore. Yes, her hips are a good size for birthing. No physical abnormalities are discernible from the pelvic exam. And then a reconstruction of her womb is projected above her belly, courtesy of an elegantly designed little remote whose circuits are imbued with tame magic, and she can't see past it. It rotates, pulsing gently, in the air.

"I see no indication that we'll have any problems with conception."

War Alchemist Corisande's expression hardens, and Lorelei can guess what she's thinking: *How far does this cursed affliction go?*

Will she even be able to carry to term? Nine hells, she doesn't want to think about that, can't think about that, she's on the verge of tears—

"I will, of course, be providing an imprint," Corisande says, interrupting the spiral. Lorelei rises up out of herself, clutching at the blanket over her lap. The older woman continues, "As well as generative force, to make sure it takes."

The doctor nods, and doesn't translate for Lorelei, who looks between the three faces in the room, pressing her thighs tight together. Her uncle is nodding, unseeing, but Corisande catches her gaze.

"That is to say," she adds, smoothly, condescendingly, "that my magic will allow me to take the place of the male component. The child will be both of ours."

I know, she wants to spit, but she can't. She didn't know. Her hand drifts to her belly, predictable and melodramatic, and she manages a nod. "Is that why you asked—"

But nobody hears her, and the doctor keeps talking. Lorelei leans back against the bed and stares at the beautiful tiles on the ceiling. She counts them. The words wash over her. Injections, she'll need injections, and of course Corisande will need to prepare her. *Harrow the field*, so to speak. The doctor assures her it won't hurt. Lorelei isn't sure she cares.

The doctor stands. Lorelei makes herself sit up, hands primly clasped in her lap. Her uncle rises too, and Corisande, and this is almost over. Just a few more minutes. She can *do* this, and not think about her mother, and how she wishes her mother could meet her children, or touch her swelling belly, or, or, or…

"May I have use of the room for a while longer?" Corisande asks.

"Of course," the doctor says.

"For what?" Lorelei asks, indignantly, when the doctor and her uncle just head for the door like this is normal.

"I would like to perform my own exam, and this seems as good a time as any," Corisande replies. She's so confident. The scars on her face glow even in the stark lighting of the room. For just a moment, Lorelei *hates* her, the way she can't hate the doctor, or her uncle, or her mother, and then the feeling slips through her fingers. She sags against the table.

"That makes sense," she says.

Her uncle does hesitate, just briefly, but then he and the doctor are gone, and it's just her and her future wife. The future progenitor of her children. Lorelei smiles up at the ceiling, baring her teeth, willing herself yet again not to scream.

"I can step out," Corisande says. "You can dress yourself. If you'd be more comfortable. It won't be a physical examination."

Lorelei stretches out a hand. "Just give me my clothing." If she's left alone, she'll break down. It's easier this way, to take her skirt and her carefully tucked underwear from Nephele Corisande, to shimmy into both beneath the blanket. She turns her face to the wall.

"I'm making you uncomfortable," Corisande says.

"Hard not to. It's nothing personal."

It's extremely personal.

"I will have to touch you for this." She sounds almost apologetic, but Lorelei assumes she's projecting; it's far more likely to be distaste. Distantly, she feels herself nod, and then Corisande's hands are on her shoulders. She can't feel if they're hot or cold, only the firm pressure, consistent, as those hands skim down her arms.

She can't help herself. She looks.

Corisande's hands are long-fingered, finely boned. Her nails are neatly trimmed and buffed. There are no fractures in her skin here, no tantalizing, unearthly blue glow;

they look expressive, sensitive. They slide over Lorelei's wrists, and then they are skin to skin, and she is cool, and careful, and silk-soft.

Lorelei's hands are clammy. Sweat-slick, clumsy. Her fingers straighten by reflex. Corisande touches every knuckle, as if she can see something Lorelei can not.

Her stomach lurches. She bites her lip.

Nephele Corisande is not distracted in the slightest. No, she is focused, drinking in every bit of information Lorelei's body is willing to give up, her gaze burning a trail over her skin, even through the fabric. Chest and belly and legs and toes. Lorelei can't help it; she shivers. She's never been *looked at*, not like this, never been consumed by sight and mind and whatever sixth sense that mages possess, that feels like a touch but not like a touch, that skims her skin and slides just beneath it, the whisper of a sensation, the promise of a caress.

"Stop," Lorelei whispers. "Oh Rifting—stop, *stop*." But she doesn't want Corisande to stop, she wants, she wants, she *wants*—

Corisande pulls away.

"Am I hurting you?"

And there's no concern in her eyes. No, it's only businesslike detachment.

Her skin settles. Her blood retreats from the surface of her flesh. "No," Lorelei says. "It was only—strange." Her gaze lifts back to the ceiling. "Sorry. You can keep going."

And so she does.

THREE

NEPHELE CORISANDE CAN still smell the antiseptic under the creosote and sugar stink of the diagnostic preparations on her workbench.

It's been a little more than twenty-four hours since she accompanied Miss Steddart to the fertility clinic. Twenty-four hours of having a lingering ghost in her head, one unexpected and unwelcome. This marriage is a matter of business and control for her prince, and access for her own research; that Lorelei Steddart looked so beautifully sad through the whole thing shouldn't signify.

And Nephele should not be remembering anything of that exam but the results: a startlingly emphatic lack of anything peculiar.

She adds a tincture of yarrow to one of the beakers, and the liquid fizzes and pops, then settles into its reaction. It will take half an hour to fully convert, alchemically, and she steps away at last, removing her gloves and safety glasses. In her pocket, her phone buzzes.

A message from the prince: *the will has been updated*.

Which means the House of Pharyn is on its way to her.

The prince had been very clear to her when they discussed Nephele stepping into the role of spouse: the House of Pharyn's assets were too great for their disposition to be left up to chance, and out of Volun's control. Nephele is loyal to the prince and only to the prince; her allegiance is simple and focused. There is no conflict of interest that Lord Steddart can object to, and with the refinement of the will, there should be no issues for the court to handle in the event that Nephele fails, and the House of Pharyn is functionally extinguished.

Nephele does not intend to fail, of course.

As War Alchemist, she is the citystate of Volun's primary military resource. Not the head of the military, no, but a specialist with the full backing of the prince, extensive education and experience, and a keen sense for the best thaumaturgical solution to a given problem. She has defended Volun on the battlefield in times of competition with nearby cities, and she has safeguarded and perfected the flow of food and other resources from farms she has helped fix in place against the wild magic beyond the city's walls.

It is her duty to keep Volun safe and hale. What is the mystery of one girl's dying family against that?

But to add marriage to the mix…

That is a new dimension. One she reminds herself is legal formality more than anything else, but it's become distracting, the thought that when she diagnoses and solves the problem of the House of Pharyn, she will be left with a wife she never planned for. A child she never expected.

It's attractive, in a dreamlike way. A strange illusion, seemingly impossible, unsettlingly immediate.

One of her assistants, Rhian, comes to her elbow. "They're here," she says. "Do you want them separated?"

Nephele hesitates, suddenly unsure of her own preferences. If they enter together, Nephele should be able to collect data about Lord Steddart as well as the niece, which may otherwise be hard to get. But Miss Steddart clearly is uncomfortable around her uncle, and he her; freed of his domineering presence, Miss Steddart may relax and be more forthcoming about her experiences.

Or they may find themselves right back where they were in that exam room.

"No," she says. "No, keep them together for now."

Once Rhian is gone, Nephele goes to the washroom to check her appearance. Limiter in place, working uniform free of stains or singes. Not as intimidating a figure as she made in full regalia, she thinks, but perhaps Miss Steddart will be more at ease because of it.

She emerges just as Lord Steddart takes a seat. Lorelei stands beside him, unsure of where to go, her hands clasped tight in front of her. Her blonde hair has been set in shining waves today, and she looks entirely uncomfortable in the outfit her uncle's staff must have selected for her: wide legged pants and a silk shell blouse with a knotted bow at the shoulder, all in that shining grief-soaked white. She looks washed out and tired.

None of the color that had come into her as Nephele scanned her body remains.

"Good afternoon, Lord Steddart. Miss Steddart," Nephele says, inclining her head.

Lorelei glances at her, then away. Nephele tamps down a strange bite of irritation. Where has the clever, angry girl from their first meeting gone? Bits of rage surface every so often in their interactions, but it seems so much further below the surface today.

It doesn't matter.

"Miss Steddart, if you could take a seat on the exam table," Nephele says, turning towards her workbench. "I have a series of preparations I would like for us to try today, which will enable us to take some baseline measurements. Do you have any allergies?"

"No," she says. Nephele can hear her climbing onto the table, but doesn't look, drawing up the first of the liquids into a needle-less syringe. Lorelei eyes the tube warily as Nephele approaches.

"You'll be less able to taste it, this way," she says. "Open your mouth, please."

ᔑᔕ

TWO HOURS LATER, Nephele has a list of measurements, all within the standard range.

Useful information, if mildly frustrating. It certainly rules out several of the more obvious options, confirming that Lord Steddart has, indeed, investigated as thoroughly as he was able to on his own. The House of Pharyn certainly has her attention now. Nephele pulls up a whitepaper on a more experimental inventory to remind herself of the procedures.

"I will need some time to set up the next experiment," Nephele says after skimming through, glancing over at her audience. "You're welcome to leave campus; there are some shops and restaurants not too far down." Her laboratory is at the eastern edge of Volun, by the walls, and quite high up. The tower is mainly set aside for state and military research, but even soldiers must eat.

"Should we keep her out of public spaces?" Lord Steddart asks.

Lorelei goes grey-faced. Nephele sets that reaction aside; it's understandable, but not something she is going to let sway her. She considers the questions on its merits.

"There was collateral damage with Fynnea Steddart's death," Nephele says.

"And in, ah, two other cases." He refuses to meet Nephele's gaze. If she had to guess, he's likely considering his own very-likely demise. "Though with Orsinil and Ruserl, the infectious illness had to come from somewhere, I suppose."

Nephele waves those two off. "Fynnea died as a consequence of her car derailing?" She knows she's correct, but she must allow Lord Steddart to feel the expert here. He's more tractable when he thinks he's in charge.

Lorelei, Nephele notes idly, is staring between them with wide, lantern eyes, gripping the edge of the table she sits on.

"Oh, rifting," Lorelei whispers.

How much does *she* know? Not enough, apparently. Well, the details aren't likely to do *her* any good, but Nephele makes a mental note to address all relevant historical questions to the uncle.

"Yes," Lord Steddart says. "And it took three other lives in the process."

"Unfortunate," Nephele agrees. "But unlikely to re-occur. In the absence of any indications of *how* the misfortune is going to manifest this time, I see no reason to confine Miss Steddart."

Lorelei hunches in a little more, before a movement of her uncle's ringed finger reminds her to straighten up.

For just a moment, Nephele considers ejecting Lord Steddart from the room, in the name of seeing Lorelei's natural behavior. But then she reminds herself that Lorelei will no more 'act naturally' in front of her than anybody else in this room. The cruel truth of the observer: she will always impact that which she is observing.

"Still," Lord Steddart says, "there seems to be no reason to tempt fate."

"If you're concerned," Nephele says, "you might travel separately from her. And I suspect the demands of my research and the preparations for the marriage will keep her occupied well enough. Miss Steddart?"

Lorelei is wavering. Her color is particularly poor. Nephele realizes too late what's coming.

Lorelei topples from the table. Lord Steddart curses, but Rhian is there, catching her awkwardly before she can hit the floor.

Nephele is by her side in the next heartbeat. Lorelei's eyelids flutter as she takes the girl's weight from Rhian. She isn't quite as insubstantial as her grief and doll-dressed appearance make her look, and Nephele holds tighter as the realization that *this* is to be her wife washes over her with the full weight of physicality. Not just a puzzle to be solved, not just a problem to be handled: a woman, overwhelmed and terrified and so very alone.

Another moment and Nephele pushes the feeling aside. She stands with Lorelei in her arms, then lays her out gently on the work table. Lorelei's eyelids are fluttering, and the swoon appears to be purely emotional, and passing off fast. Still, Nephele flicks a glance to Rhian, and Rhian retrieves the collimiting arcanic polarimeter and moves it swiftly along the center line of Lorelei's body.

Its needle indicates no deviations.

Once again, nothing of note. The disappointment must show on her face, because when Lorelei comes to and focuses on her, her confused expression quickly turns apologetic.

"I—I'm sorry, I don't know what happened," Lorelei says, pushing herself up and looking between Nephele and her uncle. "I must not have had enough to eat at breakfast…?"

Lord Steddart mutters something to himself. Unsupportive, Nephele thinks. Uncaring that the prospect of having her wings clipped by duty clearly made his niece panic.

But then again, so is she.

Mostly.

"I'm okay now," Lorelei stresses, now looking at Nephele, because her uncle won't meet her gaze. "We can get back to testing. I'll—I'll be fine."

"No, Miss Steddart. I think it's best you go home to rest," Nephele says. "We'll resume in the morning."

And Nephele leaves the room, desperate for space to think.

F●UR

THE TAPE MEASURE stretches across Lorelei's shoulders, and she holds perfectly still. It seems all she does these days is hold still, unmoving until she is posed, directed, placed. It's meant to protect her, but it feels wrong: she is vulnerable, an easy target.

But there is nowhere else to go. She's a bird with clipped wings, able to step out of its cage onto a comfortable perch, but no farther.

She has spent her days shuttled between three locations: the estate of the House of Pharyn, this dress shop, and Nephele Corisande's lab.

At the thought of her betrothed, Lorelei has to suppress a shudder.

She had thought the fertility clinic was bad enough, between Corisande's detachment and the scintillating track of whatever exam she did, but the lab is worse. Poked, prodded, all within view of her uncle; and Corisande, always there, never pawning her off on an assistant. Always watching.

Evaluating.

Finding nothing, because Lorelei is somehow failing at this, too.

What's worse is that Lorelei can't stop watching Corisande *back*. She can't understand the experiments, but when Corisande hands her something to drink, she drinks it. When Corisande asks a question, she answers it. Some of it is desperation for a cure, some of it is desperation for approval, but some of it is a desperate fixation.

Outside the walls of Volun, magic twists and churns, chaos in need of taming, chaos that can only ever be temporarily contained. But here, inside a carefully crafted ring of stone and metal, that containment is perfect. Negligible. Everything in Volun runs on magic, prettied up and gilded into mundanity. Her phone, quiet in her purse, is animated by eldritch patterning trapped on a board of silica. The glass reverberates with arcane frequency, transmitting sound and light and feeling. The railcars are powered by magic, and the tailor's sewing machines use a little bit of power to keep the fabric cooperative, and even in her old office, there was a bit of power baked into the organizational system for all the legal records, making things quick to hand.

It's very easy to forget that it's the same magic as outside, the same magic that makes travel impossible without protection, that keeps each city state its own island. That destroys, and destroys, and destroys. That is embodied so flawlessly in Nephele Corisande, showing through in the faint glow beneath her skin.

This morning, an invitation arrived: an exhibition for the prince, his War Alchemist on display in an arena against offerings from Volun's greatest artificers. Lorelei isn't sure if she's excited for or dreading it.

War Alchemist is not a vanity title. How many people has Corisande killed, in Volun's various altercations with those neighboring islands? For every sanitized opponent she will face, are there ten lives? A hundred?

Nephele Corisande is an unstoppable force, a world-ending weapon, a calamity in the shape of a fiancée.

A word from the tailor; she turns obligingly. The heavy fabric draping across her body is the half-realized form of an engagement dress. A lovely yoke to wear in two days' time, pinned in place. It needs a jacket, her uncle had decided, and so it will have a jacket. More tweaks. A few murmured comments, though Lorelei is too distant to hear any of them.

And then she's alone.

Lorelei stares at herself in the mirror.

She's lost weight in the last few months. Her collarbones jut out in uncomfortable waves, and she feels three steps to the left of her body. Grief destroys the appetite, and so does unreality, the endless certainty that this isn't her, that every moment she wakes into is a nightmare where she can't quite remember how she got there. There is blue, now, worked into the endless white of mourning garb, because she can't be mourning by the time she marries, now can she? Her hair is its natural color again, dirty blonde, but flipped and twisted and bound at the nape of her neck, polished into gold, unrecognizable.

She misses her candyfloss pink hair. She misses hand-me-down dresses and comfortable shoes. Even misses the endless, pointless grind of her nine to five office job, her flat with two roommates, how it felt to economize on groceries toward the end of each pay period. The occasional uncertainty over what would be stocked, if the shipments had come in on time, or if there'd been another supply chain disruption. The House of Pharyn doesn't have to worry about any of that.

She just wants to feel normal, for a day, an hour, a single minute.

But instead, her hip is sore from the morning's 'priming' injection, she carries some kind of death curse on her shoulders, and she's going to marry a living weapon in just a month.

Her vision turns grey and clotting at the edges, and this time, she realizes what's happening: another swoon, another faint, another desperate scream of her body against what's happening. Standing still isn't enough. It isn't going to save her.

She can't do this.

She pulls back the curtain, clutching her purse and the pinned dress to herself, not wasting time by getting back into her own clothing. It's a straight shot from the corner she's in to the back door, and the tailor is too busy talking to her uncle, her uncle too busy ignoring her as he always does. She keeps her breathing constrained, silent, as she dashes barefoot to the door, out, into the back alley.

She's not familiar with this part of Volun, but the benefit of wealth is wide boulevards and legible signs. It doesn't take long until she spots a station whose train number she knows. She has enough change in her purse for the fare, left over from a long-forgotten lunch a few months ago, secreted into a wallet that is now otherwise empty but for cards bearing her house name, that allow her to buy on credit, but also allow her uncle to know exactly where she's been, if he cares to ask.

The train comes only five minutes later. Barely enough time for her to panic.

Inside, she hunches forward in her seat, as if that will conceal her bare shoulders, the exposed seams of her dress, the luxurious spill of fabric over her knees. She took this train to work and back five days a week, but everything is wrong. It's a different car, one with seats less worn out by the commute, filled with people she's never seen. It's going the wrong way, spiraling down along the tower edge instead of up. And then there's her, reflected in the window across from her as they duck into a valley between tall buildings, *wrong wrong wrong*.

What if the train derails, like Fynnea Steddart's railcar?

What if, because she's here, a plague sweeps through this compartment? It's not crowded, but there's a small family at the other end. Corisande still has no answers, and her only reassurances are statistical likelihoods.

But the next stop comes, and she doesn't get up. Again and again, she stays locked where she is, until, at last, the train reaches its final stop. She staggers out, and the wind here is cutting. This line ends at one of the perimeter walls. There's a small fee to pay to climb the many flights of stairs. She pays it.

She's shaking by the time she gets to the top, from exertion and cold both. There are very few other people here, and below her, stretching away as far as the eye can see, are the deceptively beautiful plains of Volun. To look at them, you'd never know that they're fractured, irreparably, by magic.

Like her, she thinks. Like her.

Her phone vibrates incessantly in her purse, an angry snake, her uncle calling and calling and calling, and for just a second, Lorelei considers throwing the whole purse over the wall. It might be gone before it ever hits the ground. They'll find her, eventually, and buy her a new purse, a new phone, and she could repeat this, over and over again. The House of Pharyn will never run out of money. If it gets bad enough, she wonders, would they find a way to leash her?

Would that be any better? Take away the illusion of choice, and maybe, *maybe*, she could settle in and survive it.

Her purse goes still. She exhales, shakily, and sags against the railing, head bowed. Her skin is so cold that the sharp knife pain of the wind is blunted now. Her flesh feels thickened. Numb.

Lorelei likes to think that her mother would've gotten her out of the city, somehow, or otherwise stood up to her uncle, but no. If her mother were still alive, she wouldn't be able to stop any of this, either. No, she would've agreed to all of this. Not because she cared about the House of Pharyn, but because she cared about Lorelei, and staying the course is the only path that leads to a happy ending.

(For certain values of happy.)

(A living ending, perhaps.)

She can't withstand the cold, and she retreats down the steps, fishing out her phone at last. She calls her uncle back. It takes maybe ten minutes for him to appear, stepping out of his personal railcar. He gestures her in. She climbs inside.

"This never happened," her uncle says, tucking his coat around her shoulders. "You didn't insult the war alchemist by running away. Can we agree on that?"

Can we change reality by wishing it so, just this once?

She can't speak, and her uncle's expression softens. She sees a flash of pity in his eyes, then only sadness. "I know this isn't what you wanted," he murmurs.

"Can't you take a new wife?" she asks. "I don't—I never—"

"I can't do that to somebody else," he says, looking momentarily horrified, face gone pallid, hands clenching in his lap.

And then the horror falls away and there's only exhaustion, only grief. She isn't the only one mourning. He has buried a wife, and children, and can see the clock ticking down on his own life. It can't be long, can it? She knows the deaths have accelerated. She's seen Corisande's chart.

"But I can?" she asks anyway.

"You can do it honestly, at any rate."

The railcar pulls up outside the plaza that houses the tailor. Her uncle gets out first, then reaches in to hand her out onto the pavement. She wants to bite him.

She doesn't. She clutches her phone and types out a quick message. A plea. A cry of pain.

She hits send, and takes his hand.

He's right, after all. If she's death walking, then the only person who could choose to face her is the woman whose catastrophic power is already burning her away from the inside out.

They're the perfect pair.

FIVE

NEPHELE SIDESTEPS A spray of rocks, torn up from the ground by the current government-darling artificing firm's invention, a spidery tangle of metal and rubber that hisses and swings its bladed tail back in her direction. She lets it close on her, then drops down and surges forward, aiming for the luminescent, oozing core she feels more than sees. Her hands sketch a quick gesture, and her skull throbs dully; the thaumaturgic force moving the construct's nearest limb is interrupted just long enough for the gears to seize in place.

Her fingertips glance the core, up under its protective shell. She waits for it to go dead, the animating energy evaporating into nothing when it contacts her greater potential.

It doesn't.

Instead, the rhythm it delivers back into her hand, that resonates up her arm, is old and strong. They've gotten their hands on a relic, some conglomeration of ancient spellwork that they've tricked into offgassing power. She jerks her hand away before the protective shell can slide down and around on her wrist, and dances back, mind racing. The construct nearly lands a blow. The crowd screams.

The rhythm of the core sings across her synapses, the physicality of it slipping down into her mouth, across her teeth. It is oil-slick in its dotage. But she has heard this song before, in the research of her younger days when she had tried to study the Rifting itself, and when the core's hum lands on her tongue, she recognizes it.

Another motion of her hand, this one accompanied by a crowd-pleasing plume of color into the air. She presses in, gets her hand once more inside the shell, and drapes it with a cancelling waveform of her own power.

The construct jerks to a halt, shudders, and falls to pieces.

The crowd erupts into delighted cheering, and she can hear her name on their lips. She tries to focus on the sound, and the pounding of her own heart, the satisfaction of a win against an unexpected challenge.

But now that the fight is over, none of it is enough to distract her from her thoughts. Her thoughts, which are full of only Lorelei Steddart.

Somewhere up in the stands of the Prince of Volun's private proving grounds, Lorelei is watching. Perhaps she is even in the prince's private box, able to see the whole wide arena.

It's all a little bit sordid. This woman—*girl*—is going to bear her children and hate every second of it. It's obvious. Lorelei hates Nephele, hates her uncle, hates the world. Her hatred is quiet, and restrained, but immutable. Nephele can feel it roll off her every second they're in proximity, an almost-physical thrum that makes Nephele, in sympathy, want to run.

But Lorelei fears death more than she wants to flee, and so she cooperates.

Nine hells, but Lorelei shouldn't have to cooperate.

It's been three days since Lorelei swooned in her lab, and there has been no repeat performance. She has had Lorelei answering questions and undergoing tests every waking moment between now and then, with breaks only for sleep, and meals, and so that Lorelei's uncle can take her to yet more dress fittings. No progress, no change in circumstance, and the tension between them is getting worse.

The next wave of opponents comes dense and fast, and for a blissful few minutes, Nephele doesn't have room to think. One after another she knocks down the animatronic targets that swarm her. Her skin buzzes with the *snap snap snap* of each volley of force, the blue glow from her skin blotting out some of her peripheral vision. She dissolves into herself, her body turning fluid, a conduit for each blow, a conducting element. A war alchemist is not necessarily a combat specialist, but Nephele is, as much as she's also an inventor, a detective, a craftswoman. She is everything the prince would have her be. The crack and crumble of each construct is music, is catharsis, is proof that she knows what the fuck she's doing with her life.

And then it's over, and she's standing in a ring of useless bits of metal. Her breathing settles easily. Her heart barely races. She imagines the feel of Lorelei's eyes on her, and there she is, being pulled back down again into her thoughts. Nephele had assumed, going into this whole arrangement, that the puzzle would be challenging but manageable. A test of skill. A way to be useful.

Nephele doesn't enjoy being stymied.

She has ruled out the mundane, like the doctors who have gone before her; it is not a plague that has killed the House of Pharyn, and it is not poison, and it is not an assassin's malice. There is only the connection of the family. Something in the blood, if not the name. Something dogged and determined. Something inexorable.

Nephele has considered simply waiting to see what happens to Lorelei in the coming weeks and months, but though she is cold, she is not cruel, and her remit is to stop the problem, not just identify it.

It was never going to be easy, of course, but she is still frustrated.

Or maybe she's simply angry at the reality of getting married.

There's a roll of polite cheering from the stands as the representative from the firm signals that the exhibition is complete. Nephele leaves the arena, shrugging out of her sweat-stained uniform jacket as she goes. She retreats (doesn't hide, never hides) to a small outbuilding to mop the sweat from her shoulders, make herself presentable again. Her limiter chafes against her cheekbones; as she's aged, the padding over her zygomatics has declined, and she will need to be refitted soon. For now, she just slips a chilly finger up between metal and flesh and rubs, trying not to think of Lorelei Steddart's weight in her arms.

There's a knock at the door. Or the frame, really, from the sound. "Yes, my prince?" Nephele asks, looking at herself in the mirror. The glow from the seams of her skin is too bright in the dim lighting. It makes her look even older, more hollow.

The door opens behind her, and her liege steps inside. Alone, but with two glasses in hand. He sets one down within reach, the ice inside clinking gently, the fumes of finely distilled liquor curling up to Nephele's nose. "A good showing," he says. "Thesellia was certain they'd get you with the large construct."

"It was a clever move. I'd like to see their materials sourcing, though." It smacks of them being somewhere they shouldn't, out in the wastes.

The prince shrugs, then takes a sip from his glass. "Your bride has just left," he continues. "With permission, this time."

Nephele ignores her own glass, cocking her head slightly to one side. "And has she left without permission?"

"Ah. I see Lord Steddart didn't tell you about her half-formed escape attempt. She absconded during a tailoring appointment yesterday. Got all the way down to the walls."

Nephele grimaces, unsure if she's surprised or not. On the one hand, the girl had fainted at the thought of being trapped. On the other, it might just have easily been at the thought of collateral damage.

"This is a delicate time," she says, finally.

The prince is quiet for a stretch, then sighs. "As you say. How goes the investigation?"

"Slowly." Nephele sighs and takes the glass, knocking half of it back and sucking her teeth after. "But I'll crack it eventually."

"If you find yourself in any danger—"

"Of course."

"The House of Pharyn needs to survive in some form," the prince says. "In *you*."

He still, it seems, doesn't approve of Nephele's choice. Lorelei and her uncle clearly assume that Nephele is doing this on orders, and it's simplest for everybody that way; even Nephele prefers to pretend that's the case, now that the mystery has proven stubborn. But no, when the prince came to her for counsel, and laid out a host of unsatisfactory possibilities, Nephele had put herself forward. Had been the one to make the argument that she was most trustworthy, and the most likely to succeed in securing the prince's ambitions, one way or the other.

She'd been so certain she could do this.

She'd been so certain she wouldn't care.

"You want to go forward with this?" he asks, not for the first time.

She doesn't hesitate. "Yes." She owes him many things, but not her vulnerability. And, at any rate, the marriage is still over a month off. Propriety and event planning are still important to the House of Pharyn, even in these dangerous times. She and Lorelei will live apart until then, a final reprieve, a window of time where, perhaps, Nephele can find a way to save the girl, then give them both their freedom back.

It isn't that Lorelei is not beautiful (she is, though it's hard to tell, really, through so much sadness). But Nephele has never wanted the obligations of a spouse, and the longer she thinks about Lorelei Steddart, the more she worries about keeping an objective, impersonal distance. The finer, more human points of this whole endeavor are so alien to Nephele's existence that she doesn't know what to do. What to say. What to think.

So she doesn't. She thinks about death instead.

In that, at least, she and Lorelei are alike.

SIX

TWO DAYS LATER, Lorelei allows herself to be dressed, and primped, and displayed. She faces her bride-to-be across the shallow pool in the center of Volun Cathedral in front of an audience she does not know. This, Lorelei thinks, is the easiest moment since the boardroom, because there's a script to follow here. She and Corisande are no longer individuals. They aren't even performing; they're just the roles themselves, anonymous and repeating canned phrases that the bishop feeds them, not even expected to have memorized anything but the marks they hit.

If she focuses on the water lapping at her ankles, she barely even feels Corisande's skin against hers. It's a blessing, because she's flinched from that touch as often as she's leaned into it, and both reactions are—*humiliating.* While part of her needs Corisande to fix her, to support her, the rest of her is still reeling from the crack of metal, the bone-shaking crash of each of Nephele Corisande's victims hitting the arena floor.

There was no blood, but her mind paints the memory in lurid red all the same. There *should* have been blood. Blood, cracked femurs, and the last gasps of the dying. The absence was mere sanitation.

Corisande pretends not to notice, but Lorelei is a terrible liar. She knows it's obvious, the unsustainable push-pull inside of her, the fear of the violence Corisande is capable of twining together with a desperate need to just be *held*, for a few seconds.

Neither are on the table.

As they stand side by side in the placid pool of water, arms bound together through the intonations of the bishop, Corisande's eyes remain fixed on the far wall. Not on her bride. If Lorelei is lucky, she's only doing her job— considering perverted wards, deadly curses, a whole host of terrors. Lorelei has the ridiculous impulse to tilt her head enough to draw attention, to offer a smile, but—fuck, why would Corisande even want to see that?

So she doesn't.

And as they process out of the cathedral, the perfunctory audience heads for cars that won't take them to a pointless reception. Corisande, freed from the ribbon tying them together, keeps her distance.

"A beautiful ceremony," her uncle says, and Lorelei is too tired to argue. "Will you be resuming your work today, War Alchemist?"

Lorelei hopes Corisande doesn't see her flinch. That her reflexive, exhausted recoiling isn't why the older woman says, "No. I will see Miss Steddart in the morning."

Lorelei shuts her eyes against the wash of tangled relief and disappointment.

When she opens them again, Corisande is already walking away.

SEVEN

FIVE DAYS AFTER the engagement ceremony, Nephele
Corisande is no closer to solving the mystery, but
that much nearer to the altar.

It is night, though the citystate of Volun is not yet
sleeping. Nephele sits in the back of her private railcar,
skimming over new reports on her tablet. She has begun
longitudinal tests of Lorelei Steddart, to see if there are
any clues to be found.

There is considerable interference. Too many emotions,
too much change, and all of Lorelei's vitals swinging up
and down and around, all within the normal range for
severe stress, such that even the most promising signs
mean nothing else. Is her latent reactivity to thanatic
energy rising cyclically because of some inherent affinity
of hers to the magical discharge of death, some induced
trait, or just because she's grieving? Is her warding
receptivity fluctuating because it is not exactly what it
seems, or because Lorelei has not been sleeping regularly?

And how much is being thrown off by the medications she's begun taking, intended to prime her to bear a child she clearly does not want, except that it is necessary?

It all means nothing so far, and Nephele has a headache. Her brain feels swollen, muddy, and she can see from her reflection in the car windows that the glow beneath her skin has taken on a sickly tone. She too needs to rest.

Nephele is halfway home from her lab when her phone buzzes. She glances at it, expecting some note from the prince, or any one of a hundred mages and soldiers who need things from her on seemingly a daily basis, but it's not any of them.

It's Lorelei.

She has never texted Nephele before, and suddenly Nephele is afraid. Afraid that she has already failed, that she was not fast enough, that this girl is dying, and she—

Do you think I'll still be alive for my wedding? Serves her right, if she has to marry a pile of bones.

The fear falls away, leaving only awkwardness, embarrassment, frustration.

The girl clearly hadn't meant to send that to her. The appropriate thing to do—the easiest thing to do—is to delete the text and never acknowledge it again. Gallows humor, bitterness, anger…it's all reasonable, all to be expected. And yet she can't bring herself to delete it.

It feels more honest than any of their structured, exhausting interactions have.

Shit—Lorelei's typing another message. Nephele has to put a stop to this, has to let her know she isn't whatever confidante Steddart is seeking solace in. But before she can tap out the words, the next message springs to life.

I don't want to die.

Her heart tightens in her chest.

There is no next message. Not because Nephele shuts off the phone, but because, for whatever reason, Lorelei isn't expecting a response from whoever she thinks she's talking to. Nephele is left staring at it, far too aware that Lorelei is not just a frustrating puzzle, not just an obligation, but a person. A very scared person.

A very lonely person.

This is not Nephele's problem. Yet she still pulls up the program that shows her exactly where Lorelei is, discovering that instead of being safely at home, she's downtown. The neighborhood Lorelei is in isn't dangerous, but it is a long way from her uncle's home, and Nephele can't shake the feeling that something is wrong.

She opens the intercom to the driver's section. She gives him the address. She sits back.

In less than ten minutes, they're slowing outside a quiet restaurant, and Nephele has herself straightened out. She will check in on Miss Steddart, hopefully without making any contact; neither of them needs to deal with the other's presence right now. If all is fine, Nephele will leave well enough alone. If something is wrong, she will intervene if necessary, but most likely just call Lord Steddart and foist the whole thing onto his plate. Lorelei hates them both, but she is more used to her uncle interfering.

It will be simpler.

The restaurant is relatively new, with industrial-inspired light fixtures and a hammered copper bar taking up a large portion of the square footage. She looks for Lorelei in the booths, at the tables, and finds her at neither. But the array of bottles lined up on the mirrored shelf, like glittering books in a library, is staggering. Nephele re-evaluates the situation.

And yes, there she is, sitting at the bar, a tulip-shaped glass containing the dregs of something liquid and golden clutched between her fingers. Even disastrously drunk, as Nephele now strongly suspects she is, Lorelei has at least held onto some dignity. She isn't slumped against the bar, and she manages a small smile for the bartender when he pauses to check in on her. From the fluid, easy way he turns to unload a batch of freshly-washed glasses, he isn't on the verge of kicking her out.

Leave her. The thought shouldn't have even been articulated. She should have already turned, already left the building.

And instead, she's walking to the bar. Sliding onto the stool beside the younger woman.

"You should come home," Nephele says, keeping her voice low.

Lorelei startles, twisting in her seat to stare at her, eyes wide and shining. Her cheeks, already pink, turn red.

"How—"

"The engagement ceremony," Nephele says. "Part of the ritual placed a tracking mote in you."

That wasn't the right thing to say. Lorelei's expression crumples in panic, in despair. "I didn't agree to that," she says. "I didn't. That wasn't in the paperwork. My uncle never told me."

Nephele's suit collar feels far too tight. She shifts uncomfortably in her seat, suddenly feeling guilty. She'd thought it reasonable. But if she'd thought it reasonable, she would have made it very clear what she was doing. So she says, tersely, "It falls under cooperating with my research."

Lorelei turns away, staring at the wall of bottles behind the bar. She begins to shake.

Fuck. *Not* the outcome she wants. She rubs at her temples, her headache worsening. "I don't intend to use it unless I need to."

"And tonight?" Lorelei whispers.

"Tonight you accidentally texted me instead of somebody else, and I…" *Say it.* "I was worried."

At first, Lorelei looks like she is about to cry. And then she downs the rest of her drink and says, "I'm not dying. Not more than usual, I mean. It's fine."

And there's the spark in her that Nephele saw that day
in the conference room, that bitter perceptiveness. *Nobody
else would agree to it, would they?* she'd said, and Nephele had
realized that the confection in white knew exactly what
was happening to her.

"I wasn't worried about that," she says. Thinks of
elaborating, of apologizing for not making sure she had
counseling, some sort of network, something to offset the
strain of Nephele's work so that she wouldn't end up in a
bar, alone, drunk and scared and lonely. But none of that
feels right. It feels intrusive. She pulls out her wallet and
tosses the cash she has on her onto the bar instead. "How
much is your tab?"

"I'm fine. I'm allowed to do this for at least a little
longer, you know. I want to stay here."

"Do you, really? Or do you just not want to leave with
me?"

"You're angry." Lorelei sounds, if anything, surprised.

"I'm frustrated. There's a difference." She flags down
the bartender. "Will this cover her tab?"

From the look on his face, it more than covers it. Fine.
The man deserves a good tip for taking care of her...
fianceé.

Oh, nine hells and the Rifting, her fiancée. Soon to be,
in the most roundabout, horrible way, the mother of her
child. Nephele bites back a groan and turns her attention
back to Lorelei, who is staring at her. Her eyes are shining.
Tears? Tears, for sure. Not hope. Definitely not hope.

"Let's go home," Nephele says again.

"Where's home?" Lorelei's voice is soft.

She doesn't have the fortitude for existential questions
right now, so she stands up, twitching her suit jacket back
into place. "Where my liquor cabinet is," she says, and
holds out her hand. "You may continue to drink your way
to numbness there."

And you don't have to do it alone.

Lorelei searches her face, and Nephele prepares for the next argument. But it doesn't come. Instead, the younger woman scoots off her bar stool and grabs up her purse, then totters a few steps away. She's wearing ridiculous heels that she doesn't seem to know how to walk in. Probably her uncle's doing, replacing her entire wardrobe with more "suitable" attire without taking into account the woman who'd be wearing them.

The very drunk woman who'd be wearing them. Nephele mutters a curse and comes to her side, gently taking her arm. Lorelei lets her.

Her car is still waiting right out front. "Did you drive here?" Nephele asks, looking at the two parked railcars pulled off the main line.

"No. Train."

That makes things easier. "Your uncle will be delighted to hear that," she says as her chauffeur steps out to get their door.

"Fuck my uncle," Lorelei says, then gasps, realizing what she's just said.

Nephele is already laughing. "Agreed," she says, climbing into the railcar and holding out her hands to ease Lorelei in with her. The driver shuts the door, leaving them in comfortable darkness, Lorelei sitting only a few inches away. Nephele can smell the booze on her, but it's almost like a perfume; she's been drinking something with a lot of aromatic bitters. Vermouth cocktails?

At least she has good taste.

The car pulls out smoothly onto the main tracks.

The only lights are two low golden arcs along the ceiling, the persistent glow of Nephele's own skin, and the faint lights from the signs they pass filtering in through the tinted windows. They illuminate Lorelei's face gently, and don't glimmer off any tears. Nephele can't even see if she's blushing.

Good. Better.

"I'm sorry," Lorelei says after a long stretch of silence. "About—about texting you."

"Who were you trying to reach?"

Lorelei ducks her head. "It's stupid."

Nephele says nothing. If Lorelei doesn't want to share, there's no reason for her to push. Lorelei's allowed to keep whatever lovers she wishes, and surely has her own life that Nephele and her uncle are otherwise doing their best to rip her out of. Nephele shouldn't endeavor to damage it more.

Then Lorelei says, "My mom," and Nephele's chest tightens. "They haven't turned off her service yet. I can still...she'll never see it, but..."

"That's not stupid," Nephele says.

Lorelei goes very still.

Nephele watches, wondering if she's broken her, if she has overstepped a boundary that needed to remain in place in order for Lorelei to stay upright, stay sane, stay alive. But she still breathes. She closes her eyes a moment. Then she pulls out her phone, and Nephele watches as she selects her mother's number, and types out a message:

I miss you.

She hits send.

EIGHT

THE HOUSE GENERAL Corisande leads her into is surprisingly small, but built toward the top of one of the taller pillars of Volun, artificial skyscraping hills traversible only by steep, switchbacking stairs or the railcars whose lines spiral up around them. The vertical climb helps pack the city as densely as possible while still providing an illusion of privacy. Corisande's property resting so far up is a clear sign of status and princely favor, despite the more modest square footage.

Inside, architectural and design details reinforce the quiet opulence: beautifully patterned tile on the entryway flooring, subdued and elegant lighting, a delicately coffered ceiling. The main room has floor to ceiling windows, and though most have curtains drawn, Lorelei can still see Volun's lights glittering far below, all the way out to the walled edge of the city. Beyond there is only darkness, where magic writhes and twists the land itself, but from here, she can see all that is safe. All that is stable.

After several long minutes of staring, Lorelei realizes that she is alone. While she stood transfixed, Corisande disappeared. She tries to figure out if she's relieved, and decides the answer is a firm *not*. How strange, when just hours before she wanted nothing more than to escape beyond the walls of Volun without the fixative amulet she wears below her dress, to be swept miles and miles away by the shifting landscape, just to avoid—

All of it.

The death, the tests, the treatments, the clothes, the *marriage*. The marriage, which is so laughably unimportant in the grand scheme of things, had encompassed all of it. Had, in the last week, become shorthand for all the rest. And now it isn't. Not quite.

She realizes, suddenly, that she wants Corisande to be near her again. It was almost pleasant, their strange conversation in the car, despite the gigantic mess she was making of it all. Almost convivial, certainly intimate, not so cold as all their other meetings.

A relief. Something she might even want.

Is that wrong? Should she be fighting harder against that pull? Because as much as her skin crawls at how trapped she's become, it stills again when Corisande touches her.

She pushes the foolish impulse aside. Even if Corisande—if *Nephele* was worried about her tonight, even if she was almost gentle, this is only a business arrangement. An investigation. Lorelei is still being too sentimental and needy again by half; she's just found a new target.

She looks around; a few lights are on in the spacious, open-concept room, but overall it's quite dim. She wanders over to the nearby couch, a very minimalist thing that doesn't look at all comfortable. The entire room looks cold and barren and half-empty, no matter how impressive the view. It's a good indicator of her future.

She sits down. She wraps her arms around herself. The pain wants to come back in, despite the numbing embrace of the four—five—six? drinks she's had. It's not that the numbness is receding, exactly; it's that she's adjusting to it.

What else can she adjust to?

Lorelei is about to tip headlong back into her wallowing when something soft and heavy settles across her shoulders. She looks up, muzzy-headed; Nephele is back and has draped a thick blanket around her. The blue glow beneath her skin is brighter here, even brighter than in the dark of the car, and Lorelei realizes she's removed her limiter, the edifice of finely-worked, sturdy metal that keeps the magic roiling inside her in check. "Your face," Lorelei blurts, then winces.

Nephele doesn't seem insulted, though, and instead lifts one hand, revealing a series of interlocked metal bangles around her forearm. They are half-jewelry, half-shackle. "More comfortable for home life," she explains. "They can't withstand power spikes during combat, but they can handle sleep."

"Oh," she says.

It's startlingly intimate. Lorelei is certain the general has never been filmed without her mask, has never been *seen* without her mask except, she would guess, by her doctors. She carries too much power within her. She *is* her mask, to all the world, just as Volun is its walls.

But not at home, apparently.

And not around her.

Lorelei can't look away. Doesn't want to look away. Nephele Corisande is beautiful this way, the lower lighting softening her scowling features, her uncovered skin lending the tenderest humanity to her. Lorelei isn't sure if she wants to laugh or cry as the longing she so sternly put aside comes roaring back, cracking away her numbness for something more real.

Nephele must notice because she makes sure Lorelei has a hold on the blanket, then goes to what turns out to be a modest liquor cabinet, filled with expensive whiskey.

"I thought you'd have gotten started without me," she says.

Lorelei's cheeks burn. "I'm not—usually, I don't—" she babbles, until she remembers, vaguely, that Nephele had said something when they came into the apartment, about how she should help herself, but she'd already been too distracted by the view. "I'm good," she settles on. "Thank you, though."

Nephele comes back to the couch, empty handed, and sits across from her on the metal coffee table. She's so *close*.

Lorelei wants to say something, but there is too much between them that is too hard to sort through just now. She has been through so many appointments, tests, interrogations, and she is so tired, down to the bone. She's been juggling so many demands and hopes and hasn't let herself have many of her own.

Maybe that's where to start. To apologize for how the engagement began. To ask if—if there might be some other possibility, one that feels better, more like tonight—

"I've done you a disservice," Nephele says, cutting down all those thoughts where they stand.

"I—"

"Let me continue. Please. You are in a horrendous situation, and I have allowed it to continue being horrendous, because I can't make it not so. It will always be horrendous. But..." Here she falls silent, and Lorelei feels *seen*, because nobody else seems to care how horrible this has been for her, on every front.

She's been given so much by her change in station, and she is being looked after by the most powerful mage, the most powerful *soldier*, in a city filled with power. Sure, the price is terrible, but everybody agrees that she is lucky, too. As if the price is terrible but ultimately reasonable.

Nephele understands, though.

"But...?" Lorelei prompts, hoping for—she's not sure what, exactly. She just needs the completion of that thought, is hungry for the first time in days because of it.

"But I can, at least, see you as a woman, not a test subject. Not a job. None of this is your choice, but if you would choose to have me be—warmer—then I can..."

Silence again. Her hands flex on the edge of the table. Lorelei realizes she's nervous. War Alchemist Nephele Corisande, *nervous*. She lets go of the table and sits back, rubs a hand over her jaw. Lorelei leans forward, drawn, desperate, hoping. Hoping for kindness, yes, but something else, something more complicated. Intimacy. Partnership.

She does not want to be alone anymore.

"I'm going to protect you, as best as I am able," Nephele says at last. Her jaw is set with focus, with pride. "That is my task. It will happen regardless; I will not turn away from you. But you deserve a say in how I do that. Things can continue as they have, if that's easiest for you. But if it's not, I can try to be...oh, fuck it. You can talk to me. That's what I mean to say. I'm here, I'll listen."

"Really?" Lorelei asks. She has forgotten how to breathe. A hundred questions are crowding in her throat. *Did you choose this assignment yourself? Do you resent being made a detective instead of a soldier? Are you willing to risk your life by marrying me? If we succeed, will you resent being bound to me, to us? Will you mourn me, if we fail?*

And Nephele answers all of them when she says, "Really."

NINE

THE NEXT MORNING, Lorelei is still there. She's still there when Nephele wakes up (padding out from the guest room when she hears Nephele in the kitchen), and she lingers over coffee, over breakfast (cold bean paste buns and some almost-turned fruit), takes a shower when Nephele offers, then stands, awkwardly, toward the door but not *at* the door. Ready to leave, but not on her own way out.

Nephele isn't sure what to do with that.

It is certainly the strangest, tensest morning after she's experienced. Declaration of allegiance made and crystallized overnight, and now what? Back to how things were before?

That would be simplest.

"Did you want to run tests today?" Lorelei asks, finally. Her hands are clasped together *tight*, so tight. She needs this, and Nephele knows how to lead, so she says, "If you like."

And Lorelei all but collapses onto the couch again.

"But I thought you might want to go home first. Change. Have a moment to yourself."

The charged intimacy of the night before buzzes between them, and Nephele is still at war with herself over how much she'd bent. But Lorelei had needed it, and Nephele had wanted to give it, and nine hells, they are going to be *married*—Lorelei is going to be pregnant soon—this shouldn't be so hard.

But there's gratitude, and there's affection, and then there's *desire*, and Nephele has no idea where on that map Lorelei actually is. For Nephele's own part, she's fairly sure she's shot past *obligation*, but where she's ended up is anybody's guess.

She certainly didn't spend an unfortunate amount of time last night, alone in her bed, holding the dossier photo of Lorelei taken before she'd been forced back into her natural hair color, searching for a few measly scraps of the Lorelei she never met and will never know.

Lorelei's lips (unpainted for the first time that Nephele's seen them, a little stained still) press thin, and she looks away. "Maybe later," she says, unenthused and trying valiantly to hide it.

And why should she want to go home? Privacy isn't really on offer; she's in one of her uncle's properties. It's not *her* home.

Before Nephele can stop herself, she says, "You can stay as long as you like."

Lorelei's head jerks up.

Nephele realizes, in that exact moment, that she has never seen Lorelei Steddart look hopeful.

And she almost says, *You can stay forever.*

༄

LORELEI FUNCTIONALLY MOVES in that day.

She tries not to think about it too hard; under close inspection, it looks pathetic, a scared little girl clinging to the first scrap of real kindness she's had in months. But Corisande—*Nephele*—doesn't let her feel pathetic. She takes this all as a given, arranging for Lorelei's things to be brought over, simply assuming that Lorelei will want to personalize the guestroom she spent the previous night in.

"We have work to do," she says when Lorelei, over lunch, tries to feel out if she's really okay with all of this.

And they *do* the work. Nephele ushers Lorelei into a miniature version of her laboratory, and has her sit in a chair inside concentric rings of copper, tin, and iron. She adjusts the positioning of the rings for over an hour, stepping back to don a pair of tinted glass lenses over and over. *Looking for reverberations*, Nephele says, and tries to explain it, but Lorelei can't grasp half the concepts, so eventually she tells Nephele to just focus.

After that, Nephele has her drink a concoction containing sulfurated salt that nearly makes her retch, and then Lorelei sits in a too-hot bath for another half hour. Her sweat drips out of her, a strange and vibrant blue. Nephele doesn't come in to watch her, but inspects the bath water and the towel after she's done.

Nothing. Still nothing.

Her phone shows three missed calls from her uncle when she finally checks it. Her throat tightens at the voicemail notifications.

"I'll take care of it," Nephele says, when Lorelei finally works up the nerve to tell her.

That evening her clothing and a few boxes of her belongings arrive, and Nephele has dinner delivered. Lorelei hopes for a repeat of the night before, but she's exhausted, and is sent to bed before they've even cleared the plates. The next day, they work until lunch, until Nephele is called away to handle something at her laboratory, something that has nothing to do with curses;

a reminder that, for all Nephele's dedication, she has other obligations that have not ceased. She assures Lorelei she'll be back by dinner.

So Lorelei, not knowing what else to do, goes grocery shopping.

TEN

"**S**HE'S FINE."

Nephele's phone is on speaker as her railcar speeds away from the main army laboratory complex and back twards home. The prince's face glows accusingly up at her, though it's a static image. She's projecting, of course. But how could she not? The prince has called her, on request of Lorelei's uncle, because nobody is willing to believe that Lorelei should be allowed to make the choice of where she'll live. Very well; Nephele can throw her weight around just as much as Lord Steddart can.

"I'm following a lead. I require her to be close."

She doesn't say that everything she's tried so far, with access to her personal equipment and more privacy, has still turned up nothing. She doesn't mention how much time they've wasted talking. Or rather, Lorelei has talked, and Nephele has listened, and they've made plans to go see a stage production of *Theremont's Devotion* in two nights because why not? Either Lorelei is dying (not on Nephele's watch), or

Nephele will find a solution (and soon), so they might as well go see a pulpy musical together, eat some terribly greasy food, and have two bottles of wine between them.

I just want to feel normal, Lorelei had said, then blushed, and Nephele had been looking up showtimes immediately.

It's like a dam has opened, or a switch has flipped. Either Nephele can stand at a remove, the way she has her entire life, or she can be deep in the weeds, and Lorelei *needs* her to be in the weeds. Nobody else ever has. It's occurred to Nephele that she's lacking some reasonable defenses. She doesn't care. She just keeps seeing Lorelei texting her dead mother, over and over again, and feels again the lack of progress she's made on this fucking mystery, and—

And she can do this much, anyway.

(There had been a moment, just before Nephele had left the house, where Lorelei had touched her hand and Nephele had forgotten entirely that this girl had run away from a bloodless exhibition. Had forgotten, utterly, that any inclination Lorelei has toward her is entirely dependent on the weight of her expertise, her reputation, the possibility that maybe Nephele can save her life. It had felt gentle. Sweet.)

"He'd like details. Lorelei not coming home the last two nights was strange and unusual. Now she intends to move in with you?"

"She's under a fair amount of strain, my liege."

"She also tried to flee the city a few days before your engagement."

"Of course she did."

She might again.

Maybe she should.

Nephele's hand tightens on her phone and she fights back the surge of injured ire that leaps up into her heart at the thought. For one searing, unsettling moment, she wants to tether Lorelei to the house. To her workroom.

To where Nephele can find her, and solve her, and set her free.

This is not reasonable. This is not *rational*. She doesn't have the space for it, even less than she has the space for the initial problem the prince posed her, and *fuck*, he's talking, he's saying something, she has entirely zoned out, she can *feel* the power beneath her skin throbbing and fighting against the silver across her face. Her cheekbones feel as if they're about to split.

Deep breaths.

"My apologies, would you repeat that?"

The prince gathers himself on the other end of the connection. "I only advise," he says, "that you keep stabilizing the situation as your top priority, whatever that takes. I trust that if you're coddling the girl, it's because that's the fastest way to fixing this."

"It is," she says.

It isn't.

But she's getting nowhere fast. She can afford the detour. Lorelei needs the detour, or she'll spook. And maybe—

Maybe the path to an answer lies in getting closer.

Maybe the marriage isn't just a politically expedient maneuver.

Maybe she's tricked herself into the solution.

๑๑

ABOUT HALF AN hour after Lorelei gets the text that she's on her way home, Nephele steps into her house and stops, taking in the lit candles, her finest dishes laid out in the dining area, and Lorelei in the kitchen trying not to feel too embarrassed as she tosses pasta in sauce at the stove. If she focuses, Lorelei can even keep her shoulders from hunching in.

"Dinner?" Nephele asks, and in anybody else's mouth, it would sound mocking. Obviously it's dinner. But she sounds confused. Stunned, maybe.

Lorelei slides the pasta into a serving bowl, then takes it to the table where there are already salads waiting. The bread she fetches from the oven is from her favorite bakery, just warmed up, but Nephele's eyes widen a fraction more. This must look—excessive.

"I just wanted to say thank you," Lorelei says, once the bread is in a basket and set out nicely. She tucks a lock of hair behind her ear for lack of anything better to do. "I—is this too much?"

Nephele looks at the food, then Lorelei, back and forth, and then says,

"Marry me."

Lorelei blinks.

"I think we've already agreed to that?" she asks, when Nephele doesn't continue. She can feel herself blushing, and she sits down, tucking her napkin across her lap.

"I mean next week. As soon as possible."

Nephele isn't sitting. Nephele hasn't moved from the doorway. Her limiter is still on her face. Her *shoes* are still on.

"It's just dinner?" Lorelei says, voice ticking up at the end.

Nephele clears her throat, then opens the clasps on her coat. "It looks lovely," she says. "And I've been thinking, the last two days. We need to move the wedding up. For your sake."

"For my—what are you talking about?"

"It won't just protect your House's assets. It will also draw me into whatever is killing your family."

Lorelei pushes her chair back from the table, horrified. "No. Absolutely not. That's not—it doesn't work like that."

"Doesn't it?"

"If it did, you shouldn't have agreed in the first place.

We wouldn't need to move the date up, we'd need to *cancel* it. But it's not, it's just, it's the blood. Isn't it?"

"If it were only the blood, there would be a far greater number of widows in the family," Nephele points out, slow, patient. As if she isn't painting a target on herself. "It's the name. The inheritance."

"My mother," Lorelei says. "My mother is *dead*. After being disinherited."

"But your uncle still recognized her as family."

Nephele circles the small table. She goes down on one knee before Lorelei, and Lorelei tries not to throw up. All she can see is her mother's deathbed, now with Nephele stretched out in it instead. This isn't how she wanted tonight to go. It's terrible, wretched, horrific.

And Nephele just keeps talking. "Family is more complex than blood. And whatever is happening recognizes that complexity, can account for it. It isn't simple genetics, and it isn't limited to those named in a family tree somewhere. When I marry you, I will be a member of the House of Pharyn, and I will be on the inside, with you. Right beside you, where I need to be. That's the only place I can protect you from."

And there it is again, that childish, terrified spike of longing, *don't leave me*, but this is so much worse, now. She can't ask this of anybody. She thought forcing Nephele to spend their lives together was too much, that building a life in mockery of all the death behind her would be hard enough, but now Nephele will die too soon, too?

What if Nephele dies *first*?

What if Lorelei has to bury her?

"I can't let you." She stands, and Nephele stands too, catching her by the forearms before she can turn and flee. "I need to call my uncle," she babbles, voice rising sharply in pitch, "we need to call this off—"

"I'm happy to accept the risk."

"You're *wrong!*"

Nephele's expression hardens, the blue beneath her skin flaring, and even though the older woman's grip doesn't tighten, Lorelei freezes in place. "I am happy," Nephele repeats, voice ice, "to accept the risk. And not out of duty. Not because I have been ordered to. So do not tell me what I can and cannot do, Lorelei Steddart. I *will* marry you. And I will save you."

ELEVEN

LORELEI ACCEPTS.

Not immediately, despite the sheer force of Nephele's determination and attention. The fear is still too strong. But a little after midnight, she wanders out from the bedroom where she's been lying there awake to find Nephele gazing out at the city. She says, "Yes. I'll marry you," and Nephele raises her glass, and Lorelei can't tell if she feels relief or terror.

Probably both. When she finally falls asleep, she has nightmares.

They're familiar. As a girl, she used to dream she was being chased across a steep hillside. The chase was endless. On and on, until she flagged, until she gave in, until she gave up.

Well, she'd thought one night, lucid through a fluke of luck, *why don't I just give up from the start?*

She'd let the monster eat her, and she'd woken up.

But giving in doesn't work now.

In the morning, wrung out and exhausted, she sits next
to Nephele as Nephele calls her uncle and the prince and
outlines the change in plans. Nephele is sure and steady
and relentless, and Lorelei almost doesn't shrink down
into herself as the men lodge their objections. She almost
doesn't flee to get a shower. She's almost not grateful when
she emerges to find Nephele triumphant.

"Next week," Nephele says, as Lorelei winds her hair
up into a towel and wishes, numbly, that it was still pink.
She wonders if maybe Nephele wouldn't mind.

They spend the morning in the workshop. Nephele
has brought home more equipment, but it doesn't turn up
anything. No matter how many crystals Lorelei breathes
onto, no matter how many wires are curled around her
wrists, Nephele gets no usable results.

"And you think it will be different, once we're married?"
Lorelei asks.

Nephele nods.

"There's…something," she says. "Something near you,
or inside you. It's fugitive. It looks like random chance, or
measuring error. But I think—no, I'm *sure*—that whatever
it is is crucial. And it's so outside what I've been trained to
look for that I need to get my hands into it myself to really
understand it."

Lorelei blushes. Nephele pretends she said nothing
untoward. Then her phone pings. It's the prince, Lorelei
assumes, for how quickly Nephele retreats to another
room. She sits, as patiently as she can, until Nephele
reappears, expression set.

"I'm needed," is all she says. Not even, *I'll be back by
dinner.*

"Of course," Lorelei says and relocates to the couch.
Nephele remains in her workroom a little longer, and then
she's gone, out the door.

Lorelei watches her go and tries not to feel too much
like a puppy left home alone while its master goes to work.

The space will do her good, she tells herself. Maybe by the time Nephele gets back, Lorelei can feel grateful and happy about the wedding, can really sink into the comfort of no longer being alone.

It's not like there's anything else to do. Nephele, for all that her home is expensive and lovely, lives a very bleak existence. Few books, few recordings, and stiff furniture, barely broken in. The house of a soldier, Lorelei supposes, or at least one who has never used her rank for comfort. It's admirable, she guesses, though unpleasant, too. She gives herself her daily injection of fertility medication, then heads out for more groceries, and some light shopping. She comes home to an empty house, with no idea when Nephele will return.

She tries decorating. She tries reading. She tries watching old news specials about Nephele, but turns them off quickly when she can't reconcile the imposing, icy woman on the screen with the woman who's risking her life to save Lorelei's.

She tries to fantasize about a wedding day she wants, a *future* she wants. The warm late-afternoon, late-summer sun coming in through these high windows, washing over her curled up with her head on Nephele's shoulder, Nephele's hands trailing over her arms, her legs, her cheek. Easy conversation about nothing in particular, something delicious in the oven, music playing. Toys on the floor. A book momentarily forgotten on the cushion beside her as little hands grip at her, pull a tiny body up into the pile of them. Except then the light falters, a cloud comes between her and the sun, and the toys are abandoned, and everything is dim, darkened, fading fast.

It's not just the doomed daydream, either.

Something twists in her throat, and it's not fear or grief or anger. It's *physical*. She can barely breathe, and she staggers out into the living room, but Nephele is still gone, of course. Lorelei is still alone in this empty prison, and it's coming, it's coming, *it's coming*—

She fumbles for her phone. It opens on her third attempt. She needs to call Nephele, to let her know— what? *I'm sorry? I'm dying? It's too late? I'm so happy it happened before it could take you, too?*—but she left it on the text screen with her mother's phone, message after message of I'm scared and I miss you and can you imagine, me getting married? To a soldier?

The screen glows up at her. The world has begun to spin, but the screen at the center stays resolutely fixed.

I miss you.

I miss you.

I miss you.

Lorelei's hands spasm and tremble, but she types out a new message, one last cry into the void.

I'll see you soon.

Rationally, she knows she's on the floor now, but she can't feel the wood beneath her knees. It's as if she's floating, and the house seems to turn around her, and is this death? Is this her heart stopping? Her throat is full, her chest is full, every inch of her feels close to bursting. She hangs on to her phone. She thinks, again, of texting Nephele, maybe just to say *thank you*, one last time, but then all she can see is Nephele bursting into her own house, catching Lorelei from where she floats, untethered and dissolving into the air, bringing her back to life, and that will never happen. That can't happen. That can't…

Her phone buzzes in her hand.

The screen lights up: Not yet, dear heart. Breathe.

And she does.

One long, gasping breath, and then another. She sinks back into herself, feels her knees connect with the floor (was she actually floating? Or did she just lose track of her skin?), feels the phone pressing hard into the bones of her hand.

She's okay. She's not dying. She is alive, and her mother is dead.

She's had panic attacks before, but nothing like that. None with that level of certainty. She slides her fingers along the edge of the phone case, but she can't bring herself to look. There won't, after all, be any text from her mother there. There can't be.

Just a desperate delusion from a brain trying frantically to right itself. If she can't make herself breathe, the ghost of her mother can do it for her.

But then...what if? What if she lights up the screen and that text is still there? Shaking, she runs her free hand through her hair. Blonde; it's the wrong color, and she's sick of it. Just one more weight on her that doesn't need to be there, that's keeping her from breathing.

Behind her, the door unlocks.

She staggers to her feet, hugging the phone to her chest. The door opens, and it's Nephele, beautiful and severe Nephele, sagging against the frame just a little. Not enough that Lorelei would've noticed it in anybody else, but it's so out of character that Lorelei forgets about the nonexistent, impossible text, shoves the hangover of the panic attack aside, and drops her phone. She races to catch Nephele before she can fall.

She never gets close to falling, of course, and she flinches when Lorelei grabs her hands, but Lorelei holds on.

"Long day," Nephele says, trying to straighten, to shrug it off. But she can't. Her face is drawn, and she quivers faintly. The glow beneath her skin pulses, spikes, fades, strobes.

"Sit down," Lorelei insists. She needs to tell Nephele what just happened, but—later. Later. Nephele looks on the brink of death.

She helps Nephele to the couch, and Nephele doesn't quite collapse, but she sits, heavily, and presses a hand against her forehead.

"Do you want the bracelets?" Lorelei asks.

"Not yet." Nephele is breathing firmly and steadily, in a counted, purposeful rhythm.

"What's wrong?"

"Hazards of my profession," Nephele says, then winces. "Water?"

Lorelei fetches her a glass. She sits beside her, watches Nephele take careful, tiny sips. She remembers, again, her horror at seeing Nephele on the exhibition field. This is worse. This is far more terrifying. Is this the aftermath of magic, then? Nephele's bloodless lips, her frail form, her desperate attempts to keep all this pain hidden?

"Should I call a doctor?" she asks, finally, unable to bear up under the weight of Nephele's quiet suffering any longer.

Nephele shakes her head.

"Sometimes the magic—it comes up from the bottom. It overwhelms. The human body isn't meant..." She trails off, fingers tracing the metal over her cheekbones. "You can know your limits intimately, but still exceed them in an instant."

"We're not at war," Lorelei says. "Do you really have to—"

"Now," Nephele corrects. "We're not at war *now*. We tested a new defense configuration on some of the farms today. We need more acreage stabilized out there, in a way that keeps it safe from attack. The new approach was effective. And it was...too much."

There's blood crusted at the edge of one of her nostrils. Lorelei shudders.

"I thought I was your main assignment?" she asks.

Nephele looks at her steadily, exhaustion in every line of her face. "I have many obligations. The prince sets their relative priority. I'm sorry."

"No, that's not—I know you have a job," she says, hurriedly. "I know you can't spend every minute with me. But do you know how you look? Right now?"

Nephele says nothing.

Doesn't acknowledge that for all Lorelei knows, she could be dying already.

It's insidious, this corruption in her family. So much bad luck, so many vices spiraling out of control, so many bad decisions that should have been correctible. And perhaps that is how she'll loose Nephele: to her obligations, to the power inside of her that snaps and snarls at the leash it wears.

"It will tear you apart," she finds herself whispering, "if you let it. Maybe even if you don't. The city—the city will tear you apart." Will take Nephele from her even if she somehow breaks the curse.

"It's what I agreed to. It keeps everybody safe."

"Nephele—"

"It won't get in the way of what I owe you."

"You owe me a living wife," Lorelei snaps, before she can stop herself. Then she flushes and stands, wringing her hands. "You insist that I survive? Well, I do the same of you. We're both—we're here. Together. Aren't we?"

Silence.

"You have your loyalties, and you'll balance them. Won't you?"

Nephele nods, finally, and buries her face in her hands.

Lorelei reaches out and grasps her shoulder.

For just a moment, Nephele melts against her. It feels right good. Finally, Lorelei has done something *right* for a change. But then Nephele jerks as if shocked, and shoots up to her feet, looking around as if she's only just seeing her house for the first time. The new lamp on the side table, the art Lorelei hung. But no, her eyes slide right over those things.

"Something happened while I was gone," Nephele says.

The panic attack. But there's no trace of that, no knocked over furniture. There's only...

Her mother.

3

But that wasn't real. "I…" she starts and doesn't finish, looking for her phone.

"The wards. They're—wrong. Did somebody visit while I was gone?" Nephele's hands work, and white glowing numbers appears on the far window, vibrant against the darkening skyline beyond. Nephele draws closer to it, head tilted back.

"No." Lorelei stands too. "No, but…" Her phone lies abandoned on the floor, and Lorelei snatches it up. Nephele doesn't notice, too absorbed by whatever she's divining from the projection on the window. Lorelei opens her mouth, about to explain, about to tell Nephele that *something* had happened, something had gone wrong, something impossible had happened here.

But when she checks her text log, there's nothing but her own text of I'll see you soon.

Because her mother is dead.

"I don't know," she says. "I don't know what happened."

And she keeps the rest of it to herself.

TWELVE

THEY HAVE TO skip *Theremont's Devotion* the next night. Moving up the wedding means shuffling the social schedule means that instead of sitting in a dark, private theater box, Nephele instead hands Lorelei out of a railcar and escorts her up to a rooftop garden party stuffed to the gills with the rich and famous. They're not on one of the taller pillars; this building is closer to the wall, with a view out over the plains, and a bustling city street below with all the people walking by still visible.

She keeps her attention on Lorelei, whose hair is now a soft, curling mass of pale pink, matching the older photos from her dossier. It looks natural on her, comfortable, and it softens the otherwise alien and severe edge of her ice blue dress and diamond jewelry. The more Nephele gets to know her, the more she can see just how much of her appearance is her uncle playing dress up with her. Nephele doesn't know exactly what moved Lorelei to redye her hair this morning, without even asking Nephele if she thought it was a good idea, but she's glad of it.

Lorelei has a spine; it's time she rediscovered it.

Lord Steddart doesn't agree, if the tightening of his mouth and the narrowing of his eyes when he sees them is anything to go by. But then his gaze drops, and he must see how comfortably Lorelei is tucked against Nephele's side, because he gets control of himself. This is certainly not how he anticipated this marriage ploy to go, but he's a reasonable man. He'll adjust.

"Everybody's staring," Lorelei whispers.

"We're the strange and the new," Nephele replies. She wants to say that she's used to this, reassure Lorelei that it will pass, but it turns out there's a vast gulf between being the prince's pet tiger and now being engaged to an ascended unknown. The whispers have a different tone to them. The gazes have gone from respectfully awed to predatory, judgmental, calculating.

"They expect a show," Lorelei says, and her hand tightens on Nephele's uniform sleeve.

"We do not have to give them one," Nephele says. "Unless you want to."

Lorelei's lips purse. "I'll have to meet them all," she says, finally. "Even if I'm only to be a broodmare."

Nephele scowls before she can stop herself, and, with a few pointed nods at the guests who try to catch her attention, she shepherds Lorelei off to a quieter, emptier part of the garden. "Don't talk about yourself that way," she murmurs.

"But it's true." Lorelei is smiling, tremulous but decisive, when Nephele glances down at her. "And it's better than actually needing to be the heir to the House of Pharyn. I'm not…I couldn't do that. Even if I wanted to." They pass a waiter, and she takes a glass of champagne. Nephele slows long enough to do the same, but doesn't falter, keeping them moving until they're alone. No more observers.

"You will learn," Nephele says. "But you don't need to learn now."

Lorelei looks up at her, and her gaze shimmers, as if the stars are captured in the pools of her irises.

"I'm sorry," she says.

"For what?"

"You don't want to be an heir to the House of Pharyn any more than I do. Am I right?"

Nephele hesitates, then nods. "But duty is duty," she says. "And it is a small price to pay."

Lorelei's eyelids flutter. It takes a moment for Nephele to place the expression on her face: shy delight.

"Oh," she says.

Lorelei deserves to enjoy this: the deepening glow of the setting sun, the almost delicate distortion effect on the hills outside the wall, the floating, glimmering lights that spring to life overhead as the evening draws down. She deserves to enjoy the champagne she's holding in one hand, the passed canapés, the live music that comes, unobtrusively, from the far corner of the garden.

She deserves to enjoy this, and to be looked at and admired, and Nephele lets herself, for just a moment, feel *proud* that she has this young woman on her arm. For just a moment, she forgets their circumstances, and wills Lorelei to forget them, too.

And maybe she does. She looks up at Nephele with a soft smile. She holds out her glass, and Nephele clinks hers to it, and Lorelei says, "To us, then."

They drink together, small sips, and Nephele can't look away. Warmth blooms beneath her ribs, almost like the surge of power she draws on in battle, but entirely different in its hue. That is a violent seething force; this is inexorable, like a law of the world, and Nephele feels herself fall into it. She leans in. Lorelei tilts her head back.

Maybe, for just a moment, they can be…

"Lorelei."

And the moment is gone, Lord Steddart coming into their little piece of garden, their accidental sanctuary.

"Hello, Uncle," Lorelei says, pulling away, spine straightening.

He doesn't greet her in turn. He just looks her up and down, fist around a glass of whiskey. "So nice of you to rejoin the rest of us," he says, at last.

Nephele bristles. He's still unhappy, then, about the change in plans. Lorelei leaving his household. She'd thought the accelerated marriage would make up for it, but apparently he's decided to take this as an insult.

"We have been hard at work," Nephele says, as evenly as she can. "Lorelei has been accommodating."

It's the wrong choice of word. Lord Steddart glowers at her, cheeks a deep red. "Has she."

Nephele smiles. It is not kind.

"Have I done something wrong?" Lorelei asks, and nine hells, but she is so *genuine*. Not catty at all, just desperate to fix the situation. "I know I should have called you first thing, but I thought—I didn't want to continue imposing upon you, when the war alchemist was willing to put me up. And it has helped her research."

That shakes him a little. He looks between the two of them, and for a moment, Nephele thinks he'll behave himself. But no. He fixates once more on Lorelei. "Look at you," he says. "Your hair. Your...everything." He sneers it. "Do you intend to mock me? The two of you, carrying on as if everything is fine?"

"I don't understand," Lorelei says, with a patience that Nephele can't quite grasp for herself. "I have found a way to make the best of this situation. We both get what we want. The marriage, and a chance at happiness. Isn't that enough?"

A chance at happiness. Nephele's chest tightens. So it isn't her imagination. It isn't her being childishly desperate. Whatever is between them, Lorelei feels it too.

And surely Lord Steddart can't begrudge her *happiness*, when everything else continues on just as planned?

But his expression darkens more. He's red-cheeked. Drunker than she judged. He stalks past them over to the garden wall, gazing down at the street below as his jaw works, as his brow furrows deeper and deeper.

"And now," Lorelei says, her patience fracturing. She hurries after him. *Don't*, Nephele wants to say, but doesn't, keeping back, trying to afford them both some space. "Now you don't have to worry about me anymore."

"I would prefer," he spits, "to have never had to worry about you at all. I would *prefer* that Gwyndoffir had *her* chance at happiness."

Lorelei's mouth drops open. The last dregs of her champagne splash onto the sedum lawn, the glass only narrowly not following after. Nephele's polite smile turns fierce, and she sets her own glass aside on a nearby table.

"So would I," Lorelei says, softly, and Nephele can't be sure Lord Steddart even hears her. "I only meant—"

"Where was the prince six months ago? It was only *a family matter*, and *so unfortunate, Lord Steddart*, and now here you are, you ungrateful bastard, taking everything in hand and proudly declaring yourself *happy*—"

He is too close to the wall. He's too drunk. He lurches forward, as if to grab Lorelei, and Nephele draws up beside her bride, because he will not touch her. He will not hurt her more than he already has. He sees her, snarls, turns away at the last second.

And then he stumbles.

He collides with the wall.

He begins to tip.

"Uncle!"

Lorelei reaches for him, but Nephele shoves her back, leaping those last few feet herself. She's too late. He's falling, falling, and the retaining wall somehow isn't high enough to keep him in, and Nephele slams into that wall and grips the stone to keep herself from jumping after.

She reaches out with magic instead, tries to gel the very air around him to at least break his fall, but her power slides off him like water on oil. *No no NO, I will not allow it, I can't,* but there is nothing she can do, and he has finally remembered to scream.

And then he hits the ground, and there is only silence.

THIRTEEN

THEY SIT SIDE by side, not touching, for the whole duration of the funeral.

Lorelei is meant to say something, but she can't. Can't find the words, can't stand in front of this crowd, can't even remember how to get out of her chair. The Prince of Volun takes her place, and she can't lift her head long enough to figure out if the look he shoots her is sympathetic or disgusted. She doesn't notice many details that day. Not the flowers, or the sermon, or the scent of the incense. Later, she won't even be able to say with any certainty what she wore.

White. She wears white. Her uncle's bones are burned to ash, and she wears white and sits beside her future wife, and feels nothing.

Nothing except corruption.

It's been three days. They're hurtling toward a wedding Nephele won't allow them to move, and Lorelei can't argue against, and she has sat, for three days, as Nephele tries to work out what it is that's hunting her.

Because now they know for sure.

That night, they'd had to stay near the impact site, first because of the medics who had been called to take care of the mess that had been her uncle, and then because Nephele had needed to run tests. Tests on tests on tests. It had been cold. As the medics worked, Nephele had draped her coat over Lorelei's shoulders and asked if she wanted to go home.

"He was drunk," she'd said, shaking, huddling down into a cramped comma of a woman. "Bad luck. Just bad luck. Right? Just terrible, horrible…"

And Nephele had looked at her for one long, excruciating moment, and then she'd said, "There was something else."

Nephele should have been able to save him, she'd said, but there'd been something in the way. Repulsive and unnatural, rejecting every ounce of her power. Her uncle had been drunk, yes, but then, so many of the House of Pharyn died from accidents. Oversights, misfortunes, too many to count, too many to be just chance.

So Nephele had stayed, and Lorelei had stayed, and she hasn't warmed up since that night, frozen through and wishing she could feel terror, feel anger, feel anything but numb.

Her uncle is dead.

She is the last one standing.

⟪ つ ⟫

LORELEI TEXTS HER mother almost every hour. There is never any response, and the occasional impulse to tell Nephele about what happened the other day is smothered down into nothing. She'd had a panic attack; doesn't that sound nice, right about now?

They've signed over everything to me, she tells the void, and can't imagine how her mother would respond, even if she were still alive.

They want me to move into the estate.

We've had to order a new wedding dress. We'd tried to add some color. Now all the lace has to go, and it's just going to be an insanely expensive white shift. You'd hate it.

Lorelei can't be bothered to hate anything.

‿ϾᎧᏑ‿

AND THEN THINGS start to warp and slide.

At first, it's just her sense of time. She isn't sleeping; of course her days run together, skip ahead, stretch out like half-dried putty. She loses an hour here, gains another there. She doesn't say anything.

Nephele keeps running tests, after all. Keeps taking samples, keeps watching her, keeps *monitoring the situation*, and though sometimes she stares too long, brow creased as if she *sees* something, she never really seems to notice Lorelei's lapses.

And when Lorelei tries to be useful, *somehow*, by cooking dinner, is it really any surprise that the vegetables she got last week are rotten? They've been ordering out for every meal. Except the leaves aren't just limp, they're slick and black, and they didn't look like that in the crisper.

But magic fails, and neither of them has the mental space to care. Nephele sends out for two rice bowls, and one of her aides (because now they're not alone, now Nephele says she needs the help, and so the house is never empty) slips out the door, and Lorelei bins the rot, and forgets about it.

The aide returns. They all eat. And Lorelei reflects that she'll likely never be alone again, not between Nephele's assistants and her own Pharyn house staff, and the relentless ticking down of her own life.

Maybe that's why she wakes up that night halfway across Volun, sheltered by the jutting overhang of a darkened sign.

At first, she thinks she's dreaming. There's no panic as she stares at the lights at the end of the alley she's standing in, lights she recognizes. Lights that she used to be able to see from her apartment window. For a moment, it feels like a gift.

Then the grit of the pavement bites into her bare feet, the breeze cuts through the thin material of her pajamas.

This is real.

She trembles and checks her pockets, nearly swaying with relief when she finds her phone. But it is dead, cold, and unusable.

She edges out of the alley and along the sidewalk until she can see it, the window to her old room. There are different lights in the window now. A different tenant, with a different life.

A life without Nephele.

Her dead phone rings.

She answers.

Her mother's voice whispers, *Go home.* And all she can see is the sun coming in through Nephele's windows. The line goes silent again as tears track down her cheeks. The phone is dead. She must be dreaming.

She hugs herself tight, trying to think. How does she get from here to Nephele's? It is a long, silent walk. Peace and quiet, all that she has wanted for days, and her only company for the hour it takes to make her way up the switchback streets to where Nephele's house is. Her feet are dirty by the time she gets there, and she thinks they must hurt, though she can't feel them. Her brain is slow and fogged, but her aim is true.

And she has a lie ready, when Nephele opens the door, disheveled, hastily dressed as if she has only just awoken. Lorelei tells her that she snuck out. That she needed fresh air, and to think. That she lost track of time. Once they're inside, it already feels like the truth.

Nephele draws her a hot bath, barely concealing terror

beneath the surface. But she doesn't say anything. Not even about how far away Lorelei went, when she must have seen it on her tracker.

For once, she doesn't run any tests.

ৡৎ

AND THEN IT'S their wedding day.

FOURTEEN

LORELEI HASN'T SLEPT.

Nephele had considered slipping her a sleeping pill last night, while she bandaged Lorelei's feet. Lorelei had claimed, muzzily and without much confidence, that she'd simply gone for a walk and lost track of time. But Nephele hadn't seen her leave, and neither had her aides, and Lorelei—

Lorelei hadn't worn any shoes.

Nephele understands grief. She understands guilt, too, and fear. But she also thought she understood magic, and yet she can't even begin to construct a theory as to how Lorelei…what? Dissolved when nobody was looking, and reformed outside? Walked without feeling pain, a magical automaton that the prince would have killed to know the secret of?

Found herself flung across half the city? Her soles were certainly dirty enough for it.

But Lorelei was still wearing her amulet, the thing that sticks her in time and place in case the city wards ever fail. So that can't be it, either.

There are no answers, and Nephele, still reeling from the panic she felt when one of her aides woke her because Lorelei was *gone*, just *gone*, and the wards hadn't been tripped and the tracking mote wasn't working, could only spend the night sitting by Lorelei's bedside and hoping she'd sleep.

And Lorelei hadn't slept.

She hasn't slept much in days, and sways on her feet as she enters the cathedral where they were first entrusted to one another. She should be beautiful. Her gown is exquisite, a confection of pearl seed beads and embroidery so fine that the fabric beneath remains supple. That much work, done that quickly, cost a small fortune, but Lorelei has that now. She has been primped and polished by her uncle's staff, to his specifications, even though he has been dead for a week. The dark circles under her eyes are hidden, but she stares out, glassy and detached.

Fading, failing.

Nephele is going to lose her.

But Nephele has never given up before, and she refuses to, now. Certainly not in front of an audience. Her colleagues are here, and the prince's court, and a hundred other people she doesn't know, but that all know her. She feels the weight of their gazes as she processes to the center of the cathedral, meeting Lorelei at the font. She pours the wine, she spills the blood, she says the words.

Together, she thinks, staring into Lorelei's eyes and seeing the faintest flicker of acknowledgment. *Together*.

And when she slots her lips over Lorelei's for the first time, when she draws her wife close and holds her firm, she thinks maybe, just maybe, she can feel Lorelei sigh and relax into her. Just a little. Just enough.

"I don't want to die," Lorelei whispers.

"You won't," Nephele promises, heart aching. "You won't."

And the words glance off Lorelei without leaving a trace.

All that's left is to touch blood to blood, the sluggishly oozing cuts on their ring fingers, and Nephele keeps going, because she must, because she cannot falter, because the prince is watching and this is her duty, and maybe, maybe Lorelei will look at her again, look at her truly, look at her and *want*, like she had on that rooftop before everything went sideways.

Their skin touches.

Their blood smears.

And then—

And then Lorelei sways back, slipping from Nephele's grip, arms spreading wide.

She rises from the floor.

The audience, anonymous and omnipresent, draws back like one organism. Nephele stares, transfixed. Her mind races, then staggers to a halt, then pitches forward once more. Going nowhere, going everywhere.

Lorelei floats effortlessly, the train off her dress curling into a perfect spiral beneath her feet. The scalloped hem begins to fray, rearranging itself fractally, whorls within whorls. The whole cathedral is silent, smothered, stifled. Only the whisper of the fountain breaks through.

Lorelei begins to rotate.

For just a moment, Nephele can see her face, her eyes wide and unseeing, her rose petal lips gently parted, a light pouring out of her. It sweeps over the congregation, the pool, the stone floor. Again and again, around and around, as if searching for something. Nephele has seen this somewhere before, but this is no time for analysis.

She has to stop this.

She lunges.

Her hand closes around Lorelei's wrist, and Lorelei does not stop turning, and does not fall, and *ruin* rips through Nephele's skull.

She screams, her vision going the hot white-blue of a power surge, of an eruption, and even though she's wearing her mask, it isn't enough. It shivers in a cascade of pinging, the metal threatening to give way. It will fracture, and she will split in two. No, into a hundred fragments, into thousands of tiny, filamentous threads. So shredded, so scattered, that not even the half-mythologized Emperor Thanier could ever gather them back together.

She is lost, and she is tearing herself apart, unable to control herself, unable to let go.

But though her hand is clawed tight around Lorelei's wrist, the inexorable, inexplicable rotation goes on, and as Nephele is dragged, convulsing, something catches the hem of her cape. Her hand spasms, slips, and then she is merely on the ground. She gasps for breath, but the pain continues, unending. Her lungs struggle to expand. Her body struggles to exist.

The light from Lorelei's eyes sweeps over her. For one, blissful moment, the pain ceases. In its absence, oblivion surges in, exhaustion and helplessness overtaking her. And just before the world goes dark, Nephele finally places it.

Her wife looks, for all the world, like a lighthouse.

FIFTEEN

ORELEI SITS IN an uncomfortable metal chair. She's somewhere in the military building that houses Nephele's main laboratory; she managed to get that much out of one of Nephele's aides ten minutes ago, along with sips from a cup of water. Now she's alone again. There are no windows in this room, not even out to the hall, but every corner of the cramped space is neatly illuminated by precisely-placed glow lamps. Nowhere to run, nowhere to hide.

The walls and floor and ceiling are all worked with silver. Her wrists are shackled with it. Her head is heavy under the weight of a silver mask, like Nephele's limiter but far more punitive.

She can't remember how she got here.

She has no idea why every inch of her, bones and meat and buzzing brain, protests with each breath.

She doesn't know if she's newly married or newly widowed.

Her gaze is fixed on the door, panic and rage and grief swirling through her, and all she can do is shake with it. Her knuckles are white where she clutches the arms of the chair. She wills the door to open. She fears the door opening.

What has she done?

What has she *done*?

The door opens at last, and Lorelei jerks back as if slapped. Every instinct screams at her to run, to fight, to prostrate herself in apology.

Her voice clogs her throat, and goes no further.

She doesn't recognize the man who steps through. He's in uniform and has a small but highly-polished limiter around his left eye. Like Nephele's, but so much tinier.

"Where is she?" Lorelei blurts, when her throat unsticks itself, her voice cracking. *Where's my wife?* she wants to say, but is that for her?

"Good evening to you as well, Lady Steddart."

Rifting, but she *is* Lady Steddart now, isn't she?

Comport yourself, his tone says. She can't.

"Tell me where Nephele is, *please*." All she has left is begging. Maybe it would be better if she could sit still, lift her chin, and be the head of the House of Pharyn, but how can she? How can she, not knowing what happened, sitting here stripped of even her wedding dress? The hospital gown she's wearing drapes over her knees. There are puncture marks at the crook of her elbow, other signs of *investigation*.

The soldier considers her, weighing his answer or making some silent judgment. "The war alchemist is in recovery," he says, finally.

Recovery. The word conjures images of Nephele, collapsing in the doorway of the house. Or worse, Nephele bleeding, or burning with fever, or not awake at all.

But alive.

Alive.

Something releases inside of her, making the world wobble on its axis as Lorelei collapses back against the chair.

"Is she..." she starts, then trails off. Lorelei needs to know, but she can't get the words out.

The soldier inclines his head, waiting.

"Is she okay?" Lorelei manages, and her voice is so small. Has it always been so attenuated? So weak?

"You don't get to ask that question, Lady Steddart."

Because this is her fault. Nephele Corisande is one of the highest ranking mages that Volun has, and she's *in recovery* because of their wedding, while Lorelei is sitting chained with silver to an interrogation chair.

Rifting take her, what has she *done*? She bites back a low moan.

The door behind him is still open. He looks through it, gestures, and the aide from before (*Rhian?* Lorelei never learned their names, she was too deep in that fog of grief) brings in a folding chair for him. He sits down across from her and takes out a tablet.

"What do you remember from the cathedral?"

Her uncle would be screaming for a lawyer right now. *Don't just cooperate!* he demands in her head, a trapped ghost, an echo of a man she barely knew. *At least find out the charges!*

"Everything up until she took my hand," she says; she doesn't have the energy to be anything but truthful. Her head aches. Her eyes burn with unshed tears. She stares down at her manacled hands.

"Until your blood commingled?"

She tries to picture it, but she'd barely cared about that part. She'd still been hazy from lack of sleep, dizzy from the touch of Nephele's lips to hers. "I don't—yes? Probably."

His fingers tap at the screen, but his gaze remains fixed on her. There's no softness there at all. No allowance that this could have been a terrible accident, a tragedy, something she *regrets*. She swings wildly between contrition and fear, the suffocating numbness of the last several days, and a piercing, shrieking rage that takes all of her attention to keep inside of her.

Is that it? Is that the corruption? Is that what spilled out of her in the cathedral?

But she'd been *happy*.

For just a moment, she'd been happy. Fragile, yes, but hopeful, hopeful enough to dare to feel something through the pall of loss, and now, *now*—

She looks, again, at the shackles. They lie motionless against her skin. There's no blue glow of the kind that cracks Nephele's face. As far as she can tell, they aren't doing anything but holding her there.

"Am I a prisoner?" she asks.

"You're an unknown." *A very political answer,* her uncle's voice opines. "We're trying to understand what happened today, in order to keep everybody safe."

"Is—" Her voice catches. She pushes through it. "Is anybody else *in recovery*?"

His hand pauses over the screen, and she wonders if he'll say *that's classified* or *you don't get to ask that question.* "No," he says, finally.

Only Nephele was hurt, then; a grave crime against Volun, but the way her wife would have wanted it.

Lorelei flinches at the thought and hunches forward.

"Lady Steddart?"

"I'm glad," she makes herself say. "But I regret anybody was injured at all."

This, then, is her wedding night: hollowed out physically as well as emotionally, imprisoned, dangerous, waiting.

"What *did* happen?" she asks, as much of herself as of him.

He looks as if he's going to withhold this from her, force her to piece it together herself, but he leans back in his seat. "At the handclasping, a reaction of some kind occurred. You began to levitate. Despite never showing any magical aptitude, you disabled the war alchemist almost immediately, and stunned the rest of the attendees, until you finally collapsed."

"But everybody else is okay."

"Some claim they feel better than when they walked in. But, of course, the House of Pharyn is a desirable ally."

They're lying, in other words. *Of course they're lying.* She *disabled* Nephele—how? She can see, again, Nephele on that proving field for the prince's entertainment, dismantling constructs left and right, never faltering. How could she have stopped *Nephele*?

She twitches, and her chains rattle. She wishes she had her phone. She wishes she could text her mother.

What would she type? They're going to put me down? Worse, They **should** put me down? Or just incoherent keyboard chaos, or pleas of Don't leave me over and over again, or maybe just an apology, because she can't be sure, now, that she's not the reason her mother is dead.

If she could fell Nephele—

The soldier is no longer looking at her.

There's movement in the hallway. He's twisted in his seat, taking his eyes off her, and Lorelei tries to gather her wits, some manner of poise, because this must be an act, the next step in breaking her however they want her to break, punishing her for what she's done.

But it's not.

It's her wife.

And just as that kiss had brought color back into her life for just a moment, the sight of Nephele, alive and standing under her own power, lets loose the flood of everything she's been holding back, and she folds in on herself, weeping.

Her wife's voice, strident and firm, fills the room, but she can't make sense of it, or the scrape of the folding chair, or the footsteps coming close.

Then Nephele crouches down in front of her and frees the bracelets around her wrists from their chains.

"Come on," Nephele says. "We're going home."

৩৵৩

"I DON'T UNDERSTAND," Lorelei says as Nephele ushers her into the railcar. Her wedding dress is sitting, neatly folded, on one of the seats. She's still in the hospital gown, with the shackles and mask still on her, but she's outside the crushing weight of the laboratory and she's no longer alone. She clings.

Nephele sits just beside her, their legs touching. She's shaking a little. Her face is drawn beneath her limiter. But she is also a rock beneath her human skin. Quivering on the surface, steady at the core. "I signed up to be hurt."

"*Nephele*—"

She fixes a level, challenging glare on her, and Lorelei is cowed. She bites her lip. "They need to know," Lorelei says. "*I* need to know. Why it went wrong, how I hurt you—"

"And I'll figure it out myself. They'd be starting from scratch, and with a mindset prone to lashing out."

Nephele isn't shaking anymore when she takes Lorelei's hands and undoes the first clasp of one shackle.

"Are you sure?" Lorelei asks, flinching away. Nephele shows no trace of the panic spiking in Lorelei's chest, undoing the next clasp, and the next. The railcar hums through the city, winding its way toward the house.

"I've read over the medical write up," Nephele says, glancing up for just a moment. Her eyes and her mask catch the light from outside, sparking with color, there and gone again, pulsing as they pass storefronts and street signs. "You're no more a mage tonight than you were a year ago. You're entirely mundane."

Lorelei's fingers twitch. "That's—obviously that's wrong."

"Obviously?"

The first bracelet falls away. Her wrist feels tender, now, a pale underbelly meant to be kept safe beneath armor plates. She stares at the fluttering of her pulse.

"They told me what I did," she says.

"'They told you what they *saw*. There's a gap, between perception and understanding. What you did was magical, almost certainly. But what you did was not *magic*." The second bracelet comes off. Nephele takes both Lorelei's wrists in her hands, and she seems so strong, so sure. Like she hasn't been lying in a coma for the better part of the evening.

"How do you do it?" Lorelei asks, shifting to clasp Nephele's hands. "How do you—feel safe, after what happened? How do you just keep going?"

Nephele considers this, her thumb stroking along the edge of Lorelei's hand. "Practice," she says, finally. "Knowledge that I've fought my way through risk before. Faith, that there's a solution somewhere." Her gaze drops to Lorelei's mouth for just a second. "Sheer fucking stubbornness." Her own lips curl, like they're on the inside of a bitter joke.

Lorelei can't help herself. She leans in and kisses her wife.

SIXTEEN

THEY DON'T MAKE it to the bed.

Whatever Lorelei did in that cathedral holds no sway over Nephele's body anymore; she is strong, and unflinching, and *determined* as she peels the hospital gown off her wife's body, as she pries the mask from her face, as she explores every inch of skin with her mouth. Every touch soothes an ache, physical or spiritual, and when Lorelei begs for more, Nephele is electrified. Whole.

The army clinic feels like a bad dream. Lorelei in that chair, an intrusive thought. This, though, is real. This is hers.

Lorelei strips Nephele's uniform away with steady hands, and she must feel it too, the relief, the joy. At the very least, the wedding does not haunt her, and for that, Nephele is grateful. The work can be postponed to another day. For now, all she wants is this, Lorelei's fingers industrious and confident.

Neither of them has eaten in going on twelve hours, so they make a feast of each other. Nephele memorizes the taste of her wife, the licorice whipcrack of her own magic soaking into Lorelei's lips, the salt bite of her sweat. It nourishes her down to the marrow, and when their bodies give out, twined around one another, they sleep until morning.

Until their phones give twinned pings from their calendars.

Until they wake, and remember that today is the day that Lorelei takes on a child.

\she/

"WE CAN POSTPONE this," Nephele says on the ride over. "There's no reason to rush. Your uncle—"

"Knew what he was doing," Lorelei says, fidgeting in her seat.

"Had say in the matter," Nephele continues. "And now he doesn't."

She is so confident, and Lorelei is…something. Chaotic, perhaps. The last twenty four hours are a haze of unreality. Maybe, she thinks, she's still in that interrogation room. But no, Nephele is solid beside her, all of yesterday a bad memory, and she's fine.

She's fine.

"The House of Pharyn needs to continue," she says.

Nephele gives her a strange look, before saying, "Does it?"

Does it? The only people left who care are strangers. Allies of her bloodline, names she was supposed to memorize but never did. Enemies, too, she's certain, but she knows even fewer of those. If the House of Pharyn ceases to be, what happens? The organism that is the city may falter, but with all its number dead, is the House of Pharyn more akin to a lung or an appendix?

Fuck it, she almost says. *It doesn't matter. Take me home.*
Nephele has clearly discarded the fears and concerns of
the other mages she works with; Lorelei could finally do
the same with her obligations, and they could instead
make a nest for themselves in Nephele's home, waiting
until Nephele finds a solution or the curse finds both of
them.

But Lorelei is not brave, and never has been. "It's in
the contract," she says instead.

Nephele doesn't say anything more, not as the car pulls
to a stop and not as they take the elevator, side by side,
up to the clinic. But when they sit in the waiting room,
she keeps one hand next to Lorelei, within easy grasping
distance. If she's insulted by the way Lorelei keeps her
hands folded in her lap instead, she gives no sign. She's
just...patient.

I don't deserve her, Lorelei thinks.

Unfortunately, no matter how thoroughly she and
Nephele had lost themselves in each other last night, they
find themselves right back where they started, pinioned by
obligation.

A nurse appears in the hallway that leads back to the
exam rooms. "Lady Steddart, we're ready for you."

◟ᓇᓇᑐ◞

THE EXAM ROOM is the same as last time. She strips down
just like last time, too, though Nephele remains in the
room with her. She settles back in the exam chair, mind
racing, wondering what to say. She doesn't want to go
through this in silence. But if she apologizes, Nephele
will tell her not to, and Lorelei can't see how that leads
anywhere she wants to be.

"Lorelei?" Nephele asks, and Lorelei realizes she's come
close to rending the drape over her lap in her anxious
tugging.

"Don't say it," Lorelei says.

Nephele hums, and says nothing, instead coming up beside her and settling on the edge of the chair, pulling Lorelei in. The motion is not practiced. Intimacy is still new to both of them, no matter how natural it feels. But that makes the gesture all the more meaningful, and Lorelei sighs. "I'm scared," Lorelei whispers, letting her head fall onto Nephele's shoulders. "I'm scared of—what if it goes wrong?"

"You will have every support from the doctors. From me."

"No, I mean—what if birth isn't necessary before the curse…"

Nephele squeezes her tight. "We can wait," she says again. "Lorelei, we can wait."

"I said *don't*." She breathes deep, lets it out in one shaking gust. "Just tell me. Tell me you're afraid, too."

And she feels Nephele nod against the crown of her head. "I'm afraid," she murmurs. "More than I ever anticipated."

There's a knock at the door, and Nephele pulls away just far enough that they can face the doctor as she enters the room.

"Well," the doctor says, sitting down across from them. "Today's the day, then. Are we prepared?"

And Lorelei is about to say yes, when she realizes something.

"The injections—" she stammers, looking at the doctor, then at Nephele. "I haven't—"

Haven't thought of them at all. Not in several days. The doctor frowns. Lorelei's heart hammers in her chest. She's ruined this already. She's made herself a way out, just by failing. Just by not trying hard enough. Rifting take her, but she wants it, she wants the doctor to say, *Come back in a fortnight* or *come back when you're ready to be serious.*

"You're young," the doctor says instead. "Let me check."

And Lorelei swallows, and lets her check, and isn't surprised when the doctor announces, "You're primed. You must have taken enough of the course. Or otherwise prepared."

The doctor's gaze flicks to Nephele, and Lorelei could swear she sees a blush.

Lorelei bites down a hysterical laugh. Surely Nephele didn't arrange for last night to happen, but here they are, trapped by what they *did* do, instead of where they faltered.

The doctor presents them with what looks for all the world like an ivory-inlaid jewel box. It certainly doesn't look medical, until she lifts the lid and reveals a metal interior, filled with a pale yellow liquid. In the center, something cloudy. A little gelatinous pearl, barely larger than a pinhead, sits in the dish. It doesn't move, as far as Lorelei can see. There's no obvious pulse of life.

She's not sure what she expected. She'd avoided reading anything about the procedure. At the time, she'd viewed it as not really her business; more recently, she's been too distracted. Nephele would have explained it to her if she'd asked, she's sure, but she never did, and now it feels like the wrong moment.

"Are you ready?" the doctor asks.

Lorelei swallows and lies back, spreading her legs. "Yes," she says to the ceiling.

Nephele places a hand lightly on her shoulder, then tries to take it away. Lorelei grabs onto it before she can, and looks up at her instead of watching what the doctor does.

It's impossible to block it all out, though. The gloved hand against her inner thigh. A swab, into her, burning lightly. A cold metal rod following the same path.

The rod makes contact with her cervix. She hisses in anticipated pain, but there is none. This clinic uses numbing agents, unlike every doctor she saw when she wasn't Lady Steddart, and she wants to be grateful, but then the doctor pulls away, and it must already be done.

She'd barely even noticed.

"The potentiate seed is in place," the doctor says, smiling at Lorelei and then looking up to Nephele. "Are you ready?"

Nephele looks at her, and she freezes. It's not up to her, or it's not *supposed* to be, but it is. Nephele keeps giving her a way out.

Stop, she wants to cry. *Stop! Don't you know, the only way for me not to fall apart is to just keep moving?*

But she doesn't. She just nods.

Nephele comes around to the other side of the table. The doctor guides her hands to Lorelei's belly, one over her navel, the other nearly between her thighs. Nephele looks down at Lorelei's stomach, clothed, and Lorelei wonders if she's remembering last night. This morning. Or even the first visit to this clinic, the first time Nephele had touched her.

The magic is a hum in the air. A faint taste at the back of her tongue. Licorice again. She responds to it before she senses it, toes curling, fingers splaying against the exam chair. Her throat tightens, and when she blinks, she half expects to wake up somewhere else. To find that, just like at their wedding, something has gone wrong. That the two of them are alchemically incompatible, explosive.

But it doesn't happen. The blue glow beneath Nephele's skin flares for just a moment, and then it fades. The doctor takes Nephele's place, and runs the scanning wand over her belly. This time, there's no reconstruction of Lorelei's insides, but there is a soft chiming sound.

"The seed has taken," the doctor says, and smiles at them. "Congratulations."

Lorelei tries so hard to feel nothing, just like she felt nothing when the doctor was at work, but she fails. She fails the instant she looks at Nephele's face, and sees, beneath the concentration, the smallest sliver of hope shining in her eyes.

The tiniest fragment of wonder.

It ricochets through her, slowly at first as she dresses again, as they schedule a follow up appointment, as they make their way downstairs. But it picks up speed as Nephele hands her up into the railcar, growing in size until the car lurches into motion and she reflexively puts her hands over her belly.

Nephele meets her gaze, then looks away, almost shy. She busies herself with her phone, so dedicated to giving Lorelei space.

Lorelei stares at her own phone for a long time.

Then she sends one quick text:

I wish you were here.

SEVENTEEN

"**A**RE YOU SURE?"

Railcars can't approach Volun's gates, only the unbroken stretches of wall, so Nephele and Lorelei have crossed the final half mile on foot. Lorelei could have posed the question ten minutes ago, before they started walking, but she must already know how her wife will answer.

"I'm sure," Nephele says, and spares her an indulgent, private smile. "We'll learn something, by going outside the city. Even if nothing happens. And if something does happen—"

"We'll learn from it."

"I'll keep you safe."

Both answers are true. Nephele will fight to make them true.

It galls her, that she couldn't protect Lorelei on their wedding night. That her colleagues had thought it appropriate—*obligate*, even—to arrest her, to lock her away

and treat her like a criminal. But she has made up for it
in small and large ways in the days since, and this is just
the newest gesture: a pleasure cruise out into the shifting
wilds outside Volun, on one of the prince's landships. A
honeymoon of sorts, albeit one with an audience. The
main knot of the prince's guests walks ahead of them, a
different set from those who had attended the wedding.
They glance back occasionally, not sure if they should be
concerned.

A reasonable fear, perhaps, but Nephele doesn't share it.
What she knows:

The curse has made Lorelei reactive, but not
indiscriminately. Blood magic, a binding, produced a
response. But fertilizing an embryonic scaffold inside her
womb elicited absolutely nothing.

The curse is impacting Lorelei differently than any
other member of her family. Lord Steddart did not shine
like a beacon as he fell. Nobody has reported strange
wanderings across the city in the middle of the night.

The curse made Lorelei rotate and glow like a
lighthouse. Like the towers that stud Volun's walls and
shine out across the warping plains, guiding travelers
through the roiling paradise.

It's that last one that made Nephele decide to bring
Lorelei with her, despite her name being left off the
invitation.

She only hopes that Lorelei will not suffer for her
curiosity.

ა༽

THE PRINCE'S LANDSHIP is a work of art, made for
hosting parties like this one. She remembers when he
commissioned it; he'd asked her advice. On the one hand,
he could have gone ornate, gilded everything and studded
it with jewels, added ten viewing decks just to show off

the ingenuity of his engineers. On the other, a more restrained design could be just as showy; fine lines and perfect balance were expensive, after all, and was it not better to at least *appear* more humble?

He'd settled, in the end, on a third direction: not opulence, not efficiency, but sheer *strangeness*. He'd hired a sculptor to design the ship, then paid engineers to make it work. The levels interweave with one another through ramps and curving staircases, and the railings drip between levels. It's a static mirror to the strangeness beyond the decks, which look for all the world like simple beautiful landscapes until the ship trundles forward and the view changes in an instant. Day to night to evening gloaming to morning dawn in seconds, colors washing over the curved facades.

Lorelei stares out at it, transfixed, ignoring the whisper of conversation behind them, the clink of glasses. Beyond the intensity of her focus, though, she's entirely herself. No signs of magical perturbation. No signs of a reaction. Nephele is almost disappointed.

"Have you ever been outside before?" she asks.

Lorelei shakes her head, not looking at Nephele. Her hand is up by her throat, caressing the amulet she always wears. She doesn't need it here; the ship itself is warded, just like Volun is. It traverses the warping terrain by careful calculation and magical manipulation, the way Nephele has moved armies, the way grain is shipped to them from far flung fields. But Nephele would wager that the other guests onboard are wearing their fixatives regardless, just in case. They come in a hundred different designs and styles, so what's the harm? A last ditch insurance.

"They told us in school that it's because of magic," Lorelei says. "That we did this to the world. Is that true?"

Nephele settles back against the railing, facing in instead of out. "As far as we know, yes. But it happened a long time ago."

"What caused it?"

Nephele shakes her head, slowly. "Nobody's sure. But just as magic is too much for the human body to withstand unaided, it's possible that it was too much for the world, too."

Lorelei answers this with silence. If anything, she leans further out over the railing. Nephele ruthlessly quashes the urge to pull her back. She can't let her guard down; if she allows herself, she'll lock Lorelei in a well-appointed cage to keep her safe, and tell herself that makes Lorelei happy, too. That she is somehow different, better, than Lorelei's uncle ever was.

"I used to research it, actually," Nephele muses. "Trying to figure out how it works. Why it's there." But she rarely gets the time for it now, pulled in so many directions at once.

Finally, Lorelei looks at her. "Then do you know why magic exists?" she asks. "If the natural world can't withstand it?"

And Nephele can't give her an answer.

ᔕᕯᓂ

EVENTUALLY, THE LANDSHIP stops. It settles into a hollow in a valley, the sky night-blue and brilliant with a wash of stars above. A decayed tower sits just to the west, almost near enough to touch. A properly warded party might be able to reach it, if they knew what they were doing, but the ship stays resolutely shut.

All the guests congregate on the decks instead, on lounging chairs and about the sparkling, heated pool. There are even open-air beds, surrounded by gauzy fabrics, and Lorelei lies spread out on one, staring up at the sky.

She smiles when Nephele settles beside her.

"This is nice," she says. "Strange, but nice."

"I'd hoped you'd like it," Nephele says. And she looks so lovely here, though that may be the nascent pregnancy hormones flushing her cheeks. "You deserve nice things."

(*But what if*— a tiny voice whispers, and Nephele tries not to think of the small enkindled cells inside of her wife, a reflection of herself, a reverberation of the two of them. Of the risk she's put it in for her research. It doesn't matter. Lorelei likely would be relieved if something happens, if it doesn't take.)

She shifts, then, caging Lorelei in with her arms, gazing down at this girl who has been handed to her, who needs her, who is so fierce it makes the stars dull in shame beside her. From an obligation to a mystery to an obsession— Nephele can think of no finer path to adoration.

"You're beautiful," Nephele murmurs.

They have an audience, but it is a polite one. They don't look directly at the draped bed; they chatter amongst themselves or gaze up at the stars. Lorelei looks only at her. She smiles, shyly, and Nephele kisses it from her lips.

"Thank you," Lorelei says, when they part. She cups Nephele's cheek, her thumb set on the silver atop the bone. "I can almost forget to be afraid out here."

"Can you?"

She shrugs, fluid, languid, melting into the mattress. "It's hard to remember. That it matters at all. That it's anything worth mentioning."

And Nephele files that observation away, because— because it feels important.

Somewhere on the margins.

She slides one hand through Lorelei's candy pink curls, tongue peeking out to wet her lips, and she almost doesn't hear the footsteps approaching them. But Lorelei tenses, and Nephele bites back a sigh and rears up, looking over her shoulder.

(Her back protests. Her body is worn out before its time, pathways burnt through sinew; she will never let Lorelei see.)

Her prince stands, brow quirked. "Corisande," he says, cradling his cocktail to his chest. "Can I borrow you?"

Her answer is, always will be, always *must* be, "Yes."

༄

"WHAT IN THE nine hells is Lorelei Steddart doing on my ship?" hisses the prince as soon as they are in the relative privacy of his personal balcony. Nephele scowls, but she faces out toward the broken world, so her prince does not see it. "I'm investigating," she says, curtly.

"Around innocent bystanders?"

"The likelihood of any harm—"

"I *specifically* invited you, and you alone." Motion in the corner of her vision—the prince, about to grab her shoulder, force her to face him? If he does reach for her, he stops short. But she schools her expression and turns to him all the same.

"You never said I couldn't bring her." But she had known what he meant. Subtlety is usually enough between them.

She's surprised by how much her disobedience clearly rankles.

"Your wife should still be in custody," he says, shoulders and jaw set. "Everybody who attended your wedding knows that. Haven't you heard the whispers? Seen how people avoid her?"

"I've seen just as many come to gawk. But no, my liege. My wife will not benefit from being *in custody*," Nephele replies. "She's safe with me."

A muscle in his temple twitches. "And you?"

She would really prefer that everybody stop asking that question.

It doesn't matter.

"There have been no other adverse events. If anything, the incident in the cathedral will assist in finding an explanation, not hinder it. We have more data now that we did before."

The prince turns sharply away to gaze out into the evening dark. "When I offered you this position," he says, "it was because I thought you would find an answer swiftly. Not because I wanted you to become…enmeshed."

"Then you should not have offered me as a spouse." Nephele's fingers wrap around the deck's railing. She thinks of what it would be like to pitch herself overboard. Where would the world take her? What would it feel like, that wild magic thrumming through her veins?

Would it be agony, or the sweetest peace she has ever known, underneath her wife's lighthouse gaze?

"I didn't think marriage would turn you foolish, Corisande," the prince says, desperation cracking through his composure. "I need you back. You can't die here, or waste away, I won't stand for it."

She realizes then that it's not just irritation: it's *concern*. Fear, even.

She has served this man for decades now. Service, yes, but also loyalty, and a form of intimacy. She knows him well. He must know her the same.

"I'm hardly wasting away," she says, voice a little softer now. And then her voice catches, because to tell him that she cares deeply for Lorelei feels dangerous in a way she can't fully articulate.

Why can she romance her wife on the deck of this ship, but not say as much to her prince?

"If I order you to abandon this inquiry," her prince says, "what would you do? If a farm goes missing. If war breaks out with Lostonten. If I *need* you?"

She says nothing.

"Would you come?" he pleads. He even goes so far as to lean back against the railing, trying to catch her gaze. "Think carefully, Corisande," he murmurs. "Remember who you are."

Nephele pushes off the railing. "Ask me when it matters," she says, and turns toward her wife.

EIGHTEEN

A FEW DAYS AFTER the cruise, legs dangling over the edge of the work table, Lorelei says, "Maybe it really was just the grief, that night. I've done some reading. Loss of time is a known reaction. Pile enough emotional stress onto a person, and their brain tilts off its axis. Sometimes permanently, but sometimes temporarily."

It's easier now, telling Nephele these things. Now that they share a bed, now that they steal brief but heated touches, she can confess to her wandering, to her slippage, even as she tries to redefine it as *not that bad*. Even as she still doesn't mention the indistinct memory of her mother's voice on the phone.

Nephele hums, hands dancing across her tablet.

Lorelei tries to ignore Nephele's aide, Rhian, who is running a series of alchemical assays at the next table over. She'd almost objected that morning when Rhian appeared on their doorstep, but if Nephele trusts her to be here after what happened the night of the wedding, who is Lorelei to argue? Rhian never did anything directly to her, after all. Just gave her water. A few brief answers.

(A sympathetic look? Lorelei can't remember.)

"And it hasn't happened again?" Nephele asks.

"Not since the wedding."

Nephele taps in a note, then looks up at her. "Strange, for it to have stopped."

"Maybe whatever happened in the cathedral was an… apex, of some kind?" Lorelei twists her hands together. Her thumb catches on her wedding ring, and she spins the band. The scab beneath it came off in her morning shower.

"Possibly." Nephele looks past her, to Rhian, but there are no words exchanged. Lorelei tries not to squirm. Her uncle's house was full of servants; this isn't any different. "Or the equivalent of lancing a cyst. It may yet refill."

She sounds so…distracted. Unconvinced.

Or maybe Lorelei's projecting.

"Come here," Nephele murmurs, holding out a hand. She must have seen the darkening of Lorelei's expression. Lorelei hesitates for only a moment before taking that proffered hand and sliding from the table. Nephele pulls her close, Lorelei's back to her chest, and she settles her other hand over Lorelei's belly.

Lorelei tries to speak, but her voice fails her. *I haven't felt anything* is what she wants to say, but as she thinks it, she realizes what that means. No nausea. No fatigue. That means—

"Shh," Nephele whispers, lips brushing over Lorelei's ear. "Relax. Let me show you."

A cyan cloud condenses out of the air in front of them, not quite the color of the glow beneath Nephele's skin, but brighter, crisper. It pulses. There is no form within that cloud, but there is a rhythm.

"Is that—"

"Yes," Nephele says. Lorelei feels her smile as she presses a kiss to the top of Lorelei's head. "Safe and sound. And you with it."

"Oh." Lorelei wets her lips. "The—wandering.

Does it scare you?" It should, by all rights, scare *her*. But it hasn't happened again, not since the wedding. And it still feels like half a dream.

Nephele considers. "It did. I was terrified, that night. If you hadn't shown up at the door, I'm not sure how quickly I could have found you. But now? It intrigues me." She drums her fingers on the workbench in thought. "It's another scrap of evidence. Eventually, they're going to mean something.

"Just don't hide anything else."

The censure in Nephele's voice is tempered with fondness, but Lorelei still flushes. Then she recalls Rhian, too, and her blush deepens. She doesn't need to be chastised, however gently, in front of an audience.

She almost jumps when Rhian moves behind them, footsteps soft on the laboratory floor. "Results in half an hour, War Alchemist," Rhian says, and Nephele waves her off. The door opens, closes.

"You're running out of theories, aren't you?" Lorelei murmurs.

"I've been running out of theories from day three," Nephele confesses. "And maybe you're right. Maybe whatever it is has run its course. But I would be remiss if I didn't keep looking." She presses another kiss to Lorelei's brow, then steps away. "I'll go get dinner sorted. Rest a little."

Lorelei nods. "Okay."

Nephele steps out into the hall, and Lorelei picks up her phone, scrolling idly, though the news items and accumulated messages hold no real attraction. It isn't until she's looking at the photo taken of her and Nephele just before the wedding for the society pages that she realizes that this is the first time she's been alone, outside of a bathroom, since Nephele retrieved her from that cell.

(*But I'm not alone.* Her hand hovers briefly over her stomach. That brings with it a wave of emotion she's not prepared to deal with, so she drops it.)

It's good, though. It's been *good*, undeniably good. To no longer be alone, to maybe even no longer need to fear the immediate future. She has hope. She just spent a lovely day and night cruising through an impossible landscape, and she's come home unharmed. She has a wife who is brilliant and dedicated and actually *interested* in her, and all it cost her was…

Well, everything. But she's been given the same in return.

The phone is still in her hand, a whisper-thin weight. She scrolls idly through, until muscle memory takes her to her text log.

She stares at the unbroken string of messages she's sent to her mother.

One last tether to everything before.

But it's not real. It's never been real, never been something *outside* of her. Surely it's time to move on. But she can't bring herself to delete the contact, not without one last reach into the dark.

Everything's okay. I'm going to be okay. she types. Her hand shakes. She bites at her lower lip as the message goes through.

Then she taps out, Goodbye.

She pulls up her mother's contact info, her thumb hovering over the delete button.

She is going to be okay. And she'll finally have time to properly grieve, and to move on, and to start her own family. It's been reasonable, to keep sending these missives to where her mother used to be, but so is journaling. So is just talking, out loud or in her head.

But then her phone buzzes.

There's a response.

Tread carefully, dear heart.

☙❧

LORELEI DOESN'T TELL Nephele.

ভ্ৰ

SHE DOESN'T SAY anything when Nephele and Rhian
return, or over dinner, or when they part for the night,
Lorelei leaving Nephele's warm embrace to sleep in her
own bed because she needs the space. Needs the time.

Just don't hide anything else echoes like a drumbeat in
Lorelei's head as she crosses the hall to her own room, but
she doesn't turn back.

She can't.

She's not sure how she made it through dinner. The
moment her bedroom door is closed, the tears start, and
they don't stop. Her lip aches where she's chewed it raw,
but Nephele never noticed. The worst part is, she's not
even sure *why* this hurts so much. She can't untangle *is this
my mother?* from *is this the curse?* from *what else could be going
wrong, right this second?*

But this has happened before. The day before her uncle
died. She'd texted her mother, distraught, terrified; she'd
thought she was dying. But that had been a panic attack,
and when she'd gone back to look, there hadn't been any
response at all.

Except Nephele had said something had happened to
the wards.

Heart hammering, she pulls up the text screen again,
expecting that impossible response to have evaporated,
but it is still there.

She takes screenshots this time, hands twitching and
trembling. Proof—For herself? For Nephele?—for later.
But its persistence, from the workroom through dinner
to now, is proof of its own. It shines up at her, burrowing
deep into her brain, certain and demanding.

Maybe there's a perfectly mundane explanation.

Maybe the number has just been reassigned? But no,
Lorelei hasn't stopped paying the bill for her mother's
phone service. The number is still hers. There's no device
associated with it.

Nephele needs to know. She needs to know, just like she
needed to know about Lorelei's wandering, about the lost
time. And yet the moment Lorelei thinks of handing her
phone over, of showing Nephele the chat log, every line of
weakness, every desperate plea—

(*She's seen it already*, she tries to tell herself, *you messaged her
by accident, remember? And she understood. Trust her, trust her!*)

—she can't.

She can't give this up. She can't allow it to be dissected,
she can't let Nephele assign this out to one of her aides,
she can't give up this last little corner of her life from
before. Not when it's just words on a screen. Not when she
could keep this for herself, private and safe.

So she doesn't tell Nephele.

And she sends back, finally, I will.

NINETEEN

LORELEI BARELY SLEEPS that night, but there are no new messages, not even when she stirs from the restless doze she fell into just as the sun began to rise again.

So she showers and makes herself up and covers every sign that she was awake all night. It's incredible, how she can feel both guilty and energized at once. She is betraying Nephele's trust; she is certain she is doing what's best. The two sensations exist simultaneously, rubbing up against one another as she sits down at the dining table and eats the breakfast Nephele ordered in for them (or that one of the aides made; they're both here, Rhian and the other one. Niall? She really needs to get to know them, if they're going to be here so often, if she's going to be reasonable).

But Nephele doesn't notice. Or, if she does, she doesn't comment. Instead, she says, "What do you think about taking another trip out of the city?"

Lorelei sets her fork down, root vegetable hash untouched. "Where?"

"I haven't decided yet." She's not wearing her mask yet, and the effect is disarming, not only to Lorelei but to Rhian and Niall, who keep looking vaguely startled by her uncovered face. "But I thought you might like it. Just the two of us, this time."

She does like it, even through the upswell of shame inside of her. She has to fight not to look at or reach for her phone. *Doesn't matter*, she tells herself. "How soon?"

"This week, if you can spare the time." Nephele quirks a brow.

Lorelei almost laughs.

Her schedule is not her own, but it's still largely empty. She may be the only living representative of the House of Pharyn, but nobody expected her to be able to run things herself; her uncle set everything up to operate smoothly in his absence, and she intends to take full advantage of that until…until she can't anymore, she supposes.

"Can your experiments spare *you*?" she asks, and glances over at Niall, who is pretending to read his tablet, but no doubt listening in.

"For a day or two? Yes, of course. Especially if it helps you rest."

Lorelei pauses with her cup of tea an inch from her mouth.

"I know you didn't sleep last night," Nephele says, voice soft and low.

She sets the cup down, and is proud of herself for not flinching. "I've never been a good sleeper." It's not a lie.

"No," Nephele agrees. She stands and goes over to the kitchen. Lorelei stares straight ahead as she hears the clink of glass, the soft shush of a spoon in liquid. How did Nephele know? The wards? Or the tracking mote? How far does the tracking go?

Why hadn't she thought to ask sooner?

"Drink this."

Nephele sets a glass down in front of her. She must see how Lorelei startles at her voice.

"What is it?" Lorelei makes herself pick up the glass, consider the odd, opaque purple inside. Like wine filled with silt. There's only a shot's worth of it, streaking the bottom of the rocks glass.

"Something to help you rest," Nephele says.

It's like no sleeping pill Lorelei's ever seen, and her heart hammers away at a faster tempo now. Nephele watches her closely. But Nephele would never hurt her, which means this must be—benign. Alien, but safe.

As safe as any of the last few weeks have been.

"You're testing something, aren't you?" she asks. She can't look away from the glass, doesn't want to see the expression on Nephele's face.

"It won't hurt the embryo," Nephele says.

"Tell me what you're going to do," Lorelei says. "And then I'll drink it."

Nephele taps her fingers on the table. "And if I ask you to drink it anyway? I don't want any unconscious bias to influence the results."

"And my fear won't do that too?"

Nephele sighs. "I had hoped," she says, reaching for the glass, "that you'd trust me by now."

Lorelei's grip tightens. "I do," she says. "But that doesn't mean I'm not scared."

Maybe she's asking for too much, though. Maybe she has lost the thread of this relationship. Nephele wants her, yes. Nephele will break her out of an interrogation room. But affection doesn't preclude obligation, or a sense of ownership, and they are somewhere in the heady intersection of all of it.

And there is still something wrong with her.

She's still keeping her own secrets.

Nephele is about to explain, but does it matter, truly?

Lorelei meets Nephele's eyes, finally, and throws back the whole glass. It's sickly sweet going down, coating her throat, and the effect is shockingly instantaneous. Her eyelids flutter. The world grows soft-edged and delicate.

But she can still see the surprise on Nephele's face.

She reaches out for Nephele, and Nephele takes her hand, her arm, guides her up and against the solid pillar of her body.

"Thank you," Nephele murmurs, against the crown of her head, as Lorelei begins to sway. "I'll be right here when you wake up. And I'll tell you everything."

⟲⟳

THIS IS NOT a nightmare.

No monsters chasing her, no endless running. Nothing to flee from or circumvent. But she knows she's asleep. Her metaphorical legs are shaky, and the dream is sluggish to obey her, but this is not real.

She is standing in a tower.

The tower is falling apart.

But instead of falling down, the great hewn blocks of stone are spreading, floating, making an uneven lattice in the thick, hazy air. There are stairs below her, stairs she has a vague knowledge of *having climbed*, and above her is a wash of pink and purple and change. The air ripples. That she can even breathe it is a miracle.

(She isn't breathing, she remembers from a distance. This isn't real.)

A woman perches on one of the stone blocks, knees drawn up to her chest. She is draped in wine-colored canvas, the color as rich as the fabric is bulky and utilitarian. The hem is tattered. There are scorch marks on the skirt. But there is also gold braid, and a series of gleaming buttons. A glaive, propped against the stone block beside her, the join of pole to blade decorated with a snarling beast. Her face is covered from the nose up by the thick plate of a worked silver mask, and beneath it, her eyes are closed.

"Are you alright?" Lorelei asks. Asked. Is always asking.

The woman's eyes open.

"I'm outsized," the woman says. Her voice is low and sweet. Whiskey-seasoned. Enticing. "I can't contain everything inside of me."

"Me neither."

Her hand is on her belly and on her head. It's easy to lose track, here.

The woman looks at her. Her eyes are a brilliant, sharp-edged point of clarity in the dream haze. And then the woman unfolds herself, sliding from the stone and onto the platform Lorelei is on. She approaches with all of Nephele's swagger, all of her certainty and strength and drilled precision. She's a soldier. Of course she's a soldier.

She's a very *old* soldier. She smells of books and ruin. Her blood-slick palm cups Lorelei's chin. Her body ripples. Spasms.

"It was never meant to be a person," the woman says. "I'm sorry."

The woman's head falls back, her jaw breaks open, and she screams.

And Lorelei wakes up.

୧୨୧

THE SCREAM FOLLOWS her.

Everything is pearlescent white, and there is nothing, *nothing* but the screaming. Not even the sensation of it, how it strikes her ears, how it rattles her chest: just the noise, endless and reverberating.

And the pain.

It is a splitting, howling pain, the pain she felt at her mother's deathbed amplified a hundred fold. Her throat screams at the epicenter, but this agony goes beyond the flesh. It cannot be contained within her skin, and it spills out and out and out, staining and warping everything it touches. She can't see any of it, but she can *feel* it, pulling inwards, distorting, sagging. She can't hold it she can't hold it *she can't hold—*

Lorelei hits the ground.

The sharp crack to the back of her skull, down along her spine, sends the world dark, and when she blinks, color finally begins to resolve. Nephele Corisande crouches over her, eyes and scars blazing, the silver on her brow buzzing audibly. There is rain. It is inside the house. The glass has blown out, and lies in sparkling shards around her. Somewhere, there is crying. It isn't her.

Rhian sprawls across the floor a few feet away. Niall is trying to revive her.

Rhian isn't moving.

"Lorelei," Nephele demands. "Lorelei, *look.*"

Lorelei turns her head, which still vibrates and thrums with her scream, but the scream is inaudible now. It wreathes the room, it weaves into the ceiling, but it is soundless, and her lungs rise and fall in the normal order.

Her body puts itself back together.

"Are you alright?" Nephele asks.

And Lorelei laughs.

TWENTY

RHIAN DOESN'T WAKE up.

She's not dead. Not exactly, though Nephele almost wishes she was. It would be better for everybody. Simpler, at any rate.

The next morning, windows tarped, Nephele explains what she can. Lorelei sits wrapped in a blanket, mug clutched in her hands. Her knuckles are white. The tea smells like whiskey.

Nephele lets her have one sip before she takes it away.

Lorelei stares at her empty hand. She doesn't argue.

Not worth the conversation. The chastisement. The correction is enough; Lorelei is a smart girl.

"Her blood isn't flowing normally," Nephele says, as if the exchange didn't happen. "It…hops. It's not oxygenating properly, sometimes it bypasses the lungs entirely. But her heart is still beating."

Lorelei says nothing.

"The only thing that's worked," Nephele says, "is fixative magic."

Her wife looks at the cup, now set aside on the coffee table. The fumes tickle Nephele's nose even from here. Strong. So very strong. How much pain is Lorelei in? "Fixative magic?" Lorelei asks, clearly struggling to understand what Nephele is saying. "Like…" She touches the amulet around her throat.

Nephele nods. "Like that. The systems of her body are acting like each, individually, is outside of the city. Total chaos. I've never seen anything like it."

Lorelei's hands start to shake again, the way they had the night before. One spasms towards the cup. "I don't understand. What did I…*how*…?"

"I have a theory," Nephele says. She shifts to the couch, right beside Lorelei. She takes her hands. "But I need to know more. More about what it felt like. Anything you remember."

"It was the drugs you gave me," Lorelei says. "Wasn't it?"

Nephele lets go of her and glances away, the brief spike of shame she feels surprising and unfamiliar. "Yes," she says. "But the mechanism of action…"

She trails off, remembering Rhian's body limp under her hands. She'd dosed Lorelei to help her sleep, and yes, to provoke a reaction—but not like this.

Ultimately, though, it's her fault.

"I need to know what *you* experienced," Nephele says, when the silence stretches too long. Her cheeks may be burning, and her stomach may be twisting in on itself, but the blame resting on her shoulders doesn't absolve her of needing an explanation. Rhian's life depends on it. "It was mainly a sedative, but it did include etherwort, which I hoped would amplify any residual magical synchrony in your system. I had no reason to expect it would cause what it did."

"Not even our wedding?" Lorelei's eyes are rimmed in red, and the bags beneath them are even more pronounced. She needs rest. *Real* rest, not an experiment disguised as rest. It's written over every inch of her flesh.

"The only thing in common between the incidents was your levitation," Nephele says. "The screaming was new. Do you remember how it felt?"

That makes Lorelei drop her gaze. "Some. It felt like I was breaking. Like I was—too full."

"When you were asleep, or after you woke?"

"After. When I was asleep I…dreamed," Lorelei says. "In the dream, it wasn't me screaming. It was…" She trails off, then shakes her head. "I don't know. It was a dream. It wasn't real."

"Tell me." She doesn't touch Lorelei again, but she does lean in. *Believe in my sincerity*, she thinks. "Please. It may help me understand. Let me understand."

Lorelei is still for a long time, still and silent. And then she sits back, drawn and exhausted. She gives up.

"I dreamed of a tower. It was falling apart, into the sky." Her lips purse. "There was a woman." The details spill from her: how the woman had moved, how she'd touched her, what she'd said. Her silver plate mask.

The glaive with the snarling beast.

Nephele absorbs it all, letting Lorelei talk until she's spent, her mind racing. Lorelei doesn't know what she's describing, but Nephele recognizes it from her first mention of the purple canvas uniform. The old imperial mages dressed that way, hundreds of years ago. And the thick silver plate is an early version of the more refined limiter on her own face.

The glaive is more suggestive still.

It was never meant to be a person, this figment of the past had said.

Either it was a vision, or Lorelei's subconscious is swiftly approaching Nephele's own conclusion, weaving in bits of knowledge she shouldn't have. And yet Lorelei looks embarrassed. Ashamed. Horrified, of course, but that's been there since she woke yesterday, or at least since her desperate, broken laughter stopped.

"It isn't real, though," Lorelei adds, miserably, to break the silence. "I don't know how it could matter."

"But it does."

Lorelei bites her lip, then sits back a little, and there's that sliver of vicious confidence. It's in her, deep down. It steels her spine and sets her eyes ablaze. "So what, exactly, is your theory?"

"It might be possible——" Nephele says, and her voice catches. She feels strangely hesitant. Where is her courage? Her conviction? She's more certain than ever, but the words stumble out of her. "That some sort of magical event, a curse or even the same underlying chaotic accumulation that plagues the land outside of Volun, has become…condensed. Concentrated. Bound to your family, somehow, but without causing trouble until recently—until enough members died, or the chaotic accumulation grew, and a balance tipped the wrong way."

"Why would it kill us?"

"Collateral damage, maybe. Unintended consequences of a rapidly disordering magical system."

"But I'm alive."

"And you're different." *It was never meant to be a person.* "I think it can't kill you. I think, with nobody left, it *is* you."

Lorelei's skin turns a sickly grey, and Nephele thinks she might vomit. But she resists. She resists so much. She clasps her hands, the way Nephele has seen her do so many times, and then, with great determination, she reaches out and touches Nephele.

And she touches her belly.

"I'm going to kill you both, instead," she says.

Nephele stares her down. Reflexively, she wants to deny it, to leap to easy reassurances. But Lorelei is right: as things stand, Nephele and the child are the only targets available. And there is a real chance that Nephele won't be able to fix this before the chaos in Lorelei snaps around and slits her throat.

But Nephele is no coward. And she is getting close. She can almost taste the solution.

So she cups Lorelei's cheek in one hand, and doesn't reassure. She promises, instead, with all the strength in her.

"Not if I can help it."

໑൨൙

NEPHELE RECOGNIZES THE tower Lorelei described.

The pleasure barge had anchored not far away from it. There are a hundred old, ruined forts out in the wastelands, maybe more, but the prince had taken his guests there because *that* tower is the one where the old empire's greatest general, its greatest weapon, laid down her life to stop an invading army, and where, perhaps, the world began to unravel in her wake.

And that general wielded a particular weapon in battle, one that Lorelei described in crisp, specific detail.

So she adjusts her plans for a second small honeymoon, a private trip for the two of them. She doesn't claim the trip is just for pleasure, because to pretend otherwise would only cause Lorelei to retreat farther. She already flinches when Nephele touches her, not out of disgust but out of fear. Any further implication that Nephele is wasting time, or indulging her, would be met with immediate and strident refusal.

This is a fact-finding mission. She only hopes that, once outside the walls, Lorelei relaxes the way she did before. For all the answers Nephele needs, she also needs to see Lorelei at ease by her hand.

The prince has one of his assistants send over the navigation plan from the pleasure cruise, but he isn't pleased. Nephele doesn't try to assuage him. She's too old to play that game, and her loyalty should not be in question. Is not in question.

(Or at least, it never has been before, and she is still following orders. Her prince just seems to forget that he's given these, too, alongside all the rest.)

She borrows one of the prince's catamarans, one with an automated navigation system. She goes over the route with the programming alchemist five times before they set sail, and demands a tutorial on manual navigation, just in case. She hopes that she'll be unlikely to need it, but she can't assume that.

She can't assume anything.

§

"DO YOU HAVE family outside of Volun?"

There are no lounge beds on the deck of their small ship, only a ring of cushions, a steering post, and a hatch that leads below to a nook of a bed and a small kitchenette. They haven't left just yet; they sit in dock, Nephele going over every safety check and rehearsing in her mind what she'll do in case of every emergency she can think of. She's done this a few times already. She has the mental room to speak.

Lorelei is curled up on one of the cushions, wrapped in a robe that might as well be a blanket. Her hair is scraped into a messy bun, and she looks terrible. Her mug of tea sits beside her, cold, this time with no whiskey. Not Nephele's decision; Lorelei had been the one to ask, in a tight and thin voice, if Nephele could make sure nothing alcoholic entered the house, or followed them onto the ship. It must have taken a great deal of courage; steeped chamomile hardly compares.

"Most of my father's family," Lorelei says. She looks so very tired as she asks, "Do you think they're being felled, too? That they're already gone?"

"Hard to say." Communication between the city states is limited, after all. That Lorelei apparently hasn't heard anything might be simply because her father's family wants nothing to do with hers; it could also just be an artifact of communication speed. Phones don't work over that much shifting distance, and trade is kept to an efficient minimum, the risk of loss too great. Travel even moreso.

"I should probably be more worried." Lorelei's head drops back against the seat. "Shouldn't I? There's so much I should be feeling, and I just…"

Her hand touches the rim of her mug. Her fingers tap once, twice, and then she recoils.

"Are you mad at me?"

"For?"

"Endangering your child."

"Our child. And no."

"Why not?"

Nephele purses her lips, deciding that they are as ready to leave as they ever will be. "I'm going to take us out of dock."

"*Nephele.*"

Her hands dance over the controls. She steps away to make sure the mooring falls free, then focuses on guiding them out into the wastes. What is she supposed to say? That she's certain she stopped any harm before it could be realized? That she was only angry for as long as it took to get that mug out of Lorelei's hands?

"The odds that you did any damage with a single sip, this early on, are incredibly low. My understanding is that it's a binary outcome. Either the drinking ends the pregnancy, or it doesn't. It's only later that it causes more…endurable harms."

Those facts taste ill in her mouth, as well.

"I forgot," Lorelei says.

Nephele turns to look.

Lorelei's features are distraught. Horrified. "I honestly forgot," she says again. "I didn't think. I just—I *hurt*, and I didn't think time would continue on, and I *forgot*, because I still can't feel anything. Is it bad, that I can't feel anything? It's just—intellectual, hypothetical, I'm never nauseous, I'm only tired because I can't sleep,

I can't tell that any of it is *real*." The world ebbs and flows around them, and Lorelei finally looks at Nephele again. "It's real. Isn't it?"

Nephele doesn't look at the control panel. She takes it on faith that the autopilot will carry them, and she goes to Lorelei, kneels before her. "It's real."

"It's just," Lorelei says, and her lips stretch into a grimace that thinks it should be a smile, "that sometimes I feel like I've invented all of this. Some narrative to prove that I'm special, some lie to make it all okay. I can't touch any of it. I can't *see* it. A curse, Nephele? Me, some living distillation of—of—"

"Of chaotic accumulation," Nephele says, softly. She traces Lorelei's cheek, then holds her jaw, firm. "If you don't want to believe it's real, you don't have to. Take refuge in fantasy. I'll hold the course."

"But *why*?" Lorelei scowls, tearing away from her. "I can't accept your—your self sacrifice. Your endless patience."

Those words fit ill on her shoulders, and Nephele shakes her head. "I drugged you. Remember?"

"For my own good!" Lorelei's hands fist in her hair.

Their surroundings flicker by, faster and faster as the ship picks up speed. It's advised for passengers to go below when traveling at such a rapid clip. For Nephele to go below, too, because she isn't an experienced pilot. The constant shift and change and strobe of reality is overwhelming, incomprehensible. People are not made for this.

Nephele grimaces and seizes Lorelei, dragging her hard against her chest, burying her face into Nephele's shoulder. She holds tight as Lorelei thrashes, screaming into her. A mundane, mortal scream, this time; Nephele still flinches. She half expects Lorelei to take flight again, but she is solid, solid, solid. Solid and breaking.

When the screaming stops, when Lorelei's throat is raw and her lungs exhausted, when she trembles, Nephele holds her tighter still. "I'm stubborn," she reminds Lorelei.

"And I have spent my entire career hurting others. Inventing ways to do it, if I didn't do it directly. Practically a peacetime general, and yet…"

She frowns.

"This is one of the only tasks I have ever taken on for myself," she adds, softer now. "And I chose this. I keep choosing this. Let me make my mistakes, especially if they can help you."

Lorelei shifts. "I'm a mistake?"

Nephele scowls. "Trust you to take it that way. No. No, but I'd never argue that this is a safe and beautiful path to walk down."

Lorelei snorts, limp in Nephele's arms.

"Go down below," Nephele says. "Rest. In the morning, we'll be somewhere new, and we'll try again."

"Sometimes," Lorelei mumbles, "I wish I could hate you. Or think that I should. You're—immovable. A pillar that I'm chained to. But then the storm comes, and I wouldn't have it any other way, because without you, I'd be lost. Is that pathetic?"

"Pathetic? No." Nephele presses a kiss to Lorelei's hair, turning the image around in her mind. The sacrifice tethered to the rock. The rock, given purpose, made an altar. "If we are chained, it is to each other. And I'd have it no other way."

At that, Lorelei smiles. It's almost a true smile. Her gaze drifts, then, out to the wilds around them, and the shifting light bathes her face. Her eyes take on a softer edge, that same easiness from the prince's cruise.

There is something out here that calls to her.

"Go rest," Nephele urges.

In the end, she all but carries Lorelei inside.

TWENTY ONE

NEPHELE TELLS HER it will be another four hours until they reach the tower, according to the navigation system's estimates. Four hours of being cooped up inside; Nephele won't let her above deck again.

It's impressive, how Nephele can simultaneously be both caring and utterly dictatorial.

Maybe it was unavoidable. Nephele is so many years older than she is, and so used to being obeyed. So used to command. And she is, and always will be, the savior in this relationship, while Lorelei struggles and suffers and faces down death, again and again.

(*That's not fair*, her mind whispers. *She's going to die before you do. She said it herself.*)

But she doesn't act like it. She refuses to be afraid, and Lorelei longs for that certainty as much as she hates it. What must it be like, to be so fucking *certain* that the world will bow to you, if only you keep battering yourself against it?

The nook holding the bed is just a tiny box, a closet turned on its side. There's a small shelf, and a light, but the ceiling is only three feet above her, and the mattress is hemmed in on all sides by polished wood except for the little portal into the kitchenette and the stairway. She is cocooned, and she knows she should sleep. Her body screams for it as much as it screams to be above deck, overwhelmed by the wash of images around her.

But Nephele is sitting in the kitchenette, working away at some projection or other on her tablet, limiter bracelets chiming occasionally. There's no way out, and no way for Lorelei to fall asleep. Maybe, if Nephele stripped down, if they lost themselves together for half an hour…but Lorelei can't stomach it. Not right now.

Maybe she is starting to feel something. Maybe the nausea is physical.

Without sleep, without the wind in her hair, Lorelei curls in on herself even more. She takes out her phone. It doesn't have service out here, but she has a few little games stored on it, and photos, and a book she started reading just before her mother was hospitalized that she hasn't touched since.

Her screen glows with a new message.

Are you coming to visit?

It's from her mother. Impossible, in so many respects.

Her heart begins to pound. Her palms sweat. *Coming to visit*. Does that mean this little jaunt, or does it mean drawing closer to death? Her mother is everywhere and nowhere.

Her mother is on the screen.

Her mother's voice echoes in her ears.

Where are you? she sends back.

I can feel you, her mother responds. I haven't held you in so long. Oh, Lorelei, I wasted so many opportunities.

Lorelei chokes back a sob. She presses her cheek to the pillow, slides along the mattress, as if a little pressure can force out the pain from beneath her skin.

She types and sends: I'm pregnant.

There's no immediate reply. She holds her breath, even knowing it's foolish. Her mother almost never responds. Here, now, she can't even say with any certainty that the second message *was* a response. Maybe it was just asynchronous. But she wants to know, *needs* to know, if her mother is happy.

Can the dead be happy?

I know. her mother replies. I can feel them. too. They are so fierce.

And Lorelei begins to cry.

She does her best to dampen her voice, to muffle it in her pillow. She knows how to shake apart silently; she did it often enough at school, and in her uncle's home. Sand laps against the hull of the ship, white noise, but Nephele is close by. Nephele knows her. Nephele orients to the sound of her tears like a hunting dog.

"Lorelei," she says. And Lorelei whines, heartsick, and drags her phone beneath her body.

"Lorelei, *look at me.*"

No, no, she can't look, she *won't*. Nephele cannot command her. Lorelei curls up tight and says nothing. If she just says nothing, it isn't real, and if it isn't real, Nephele can't take it from her.

Just let me pretend.

But Nephele can tell when something is wrong (and Lorelei knows, deep down, that this is certainly not *right*), and she leans into the nook and takes hold of Lorelei's shoulder. She pulls, hard, and Lorelei overbalances, sprawling back across the mattress. The phone goes wide along with her hand. It glows bright in the dark space.

Nephele stares at it.

Lorelei's mother is typing.

"No," Lorelei says, and tries to retreat. Nephele snatches the phone from her hand before she can. Her mask is off, and her expression turns thunderous in the gloom.

The blue glow beneath her skin, spilling out of the cracks across her brow and cheeks, is stronger than the little light, stronger than the phone screen.

"Give it *back*!" Lorelei shrieks, lunging, but Nephele is already out of reach.

She is staring down at the rectangle of metal and glass and magic. It shivers with a new message.

"This shouldn't work," Nephele says. "This shouldn't—what *is* this?"

"It's nothing," Lorelei says, on hands and knees now, fisting the sheets. "It's fake. It's not *real*."

But Nephele is scrolling now, back through the messages, every confession, every plea. She knows exactly what it is. Lorelei told her.

And so Nephele knows how impossible it is, too.

Her voice is cold. "Something is answering you." Sharp and brittle, liable to crack into lacerating shards.

And Lorelei could agree. Could say *yes*, **something**, because it can't be her mother. She can trot out every explanation she's already ruled out. Claim to just be sad and desperate; oh, she knows whoever's responding isn't her mother, but can't she pretend? Can't she, just for a while?

It's not real, it's not real.

But it is.

"You lied to me," Nephele says, when Lorelei doesn't respond. "You *hid* this from me. Why?" Her voice cracks, just a little, and maybe if it hadn't, if Nephele had stayed strong, Lorelei could have been contrite.

Or maybe she would always have been filled with this same, searing rage.

Rifting take her, she's more upset over *this* than she was over Lorelei drinking while carrying their child.

(Of course she is. The puzzle matters more to her than Lorelei. Than their future.)

"Oh, get over yourself," she bites. "I just wanted one *fucking* thing that wasn't yours, too!"

And Nephele bristles, feeling the strike, refusing to allow it. "This is impossible, Lorelei," she says, voice low. No more cracks. Just disdain. Just judgment. "This is not natural. This is a clue, and you're smart enough to realize that. I know you are."

"It's my mother!"

"Your mother is dead."

"And *fucking* yet!" She lunges again, and this time she's able to grab the phone, wrest it back. "It's not somebody else who picked up her number. It's not a glitch. It's not real, but it is *true*, and it's none of your fucking business."

"You made it my business."

Nephele pushes into the nook, caging Lorelei with her arms. She doesn't touch Lorelei, mantling her instead, but Lorelei can feel the fizz and pop of power cascading off her limbs. She wants to throttle her. Wants to kiss her. Everything is so mixed up and above all else, she just wants to sob.

"Don't ever," Nephele murmurs against the curve of her jaw, "keep something like this from me again."

"Or else what?" Lorelei whispers.

But Nephele doesn't answer. She just plucks the phone from Lorelei's grip once more, and then she's gone, surging up the stairs to the main deck, leaving Lorelei to curl up on herself and begin to sob.

TWENTY TWO

T HEY'VE REACHED THE tower—or as close as they
can get. Even the prince's navigational charts
can't bring the ship right up against any wall, but
sometime during Lorelei's rageful begging the ship slid to
a halt. It's dusk, not quite night, though Nephele wonders,
fleetingly, if it's always waning day here. Wonders if it's
always waning day inside her wife.

Far off in the distance, the beams of Volun's lighthouses
wink and sweep along the coast.

Come home, they whisper. *Come home, come home, don't
waste your time on this.*

But that's the coward's path, and she has never (*never*)
been a coward.

She knows what to do next. Lorelei's phone glows up
at her, still unlocked, and there are the messages from a
dead woman. From, if Nephele's haphazard, wild theory
is right, some lingering impression of a memory on a
formless, thrashing chaos that is now caged inside Lorelei,

threatening to break free. If she types a message, will she get a response? Or is there some sort of alchemy that only happens when Lorelei's fingers swipe across the glass?

The possibilities should be entrancing, invigorating, but instead they are ashes on her tongue.

Why does this *hurt* so much?

Because, whatever she said to Lorelei, it's not the lying. Lying she can understand. Fuck, she can understand *this*, but it doesn't matter. Lorelei had spat *I just wanted one fucking thing that wasn't yours, too!* and it has gored her to the marrow. She can feel it in her intestines, shredding, spilling filth and exhausted bile. And her knee-jerk, knife's edge reaction is *why?*

Why does Lorelei want something that isn't Nephele's?

And when did Nephele become obsessed with giving her the world, and everything in it?

She sits and stares out at the wastes. Patchy grasslands, scarred and pitted by an ancient war. Time slips away from her. The dusk never progresses, the cycle is stopped, and the air is still and cool and empty of any birdsong. The phone remains unlocked, glowing steadily. The battery doesn't seem to drain, but perhaps Nephele doesn't sit for as long as she thinks.

Lorelei hasn't come looking, at any rate.

She remains obedient, for all her defiance. Or maybe she's only hurting, only regretting, only wondering what else she could have had.

Nephele stares down at the chat log.

She abandons all pretense.

She types, What do you want with her?

She hits send.

There is no answer.

Maybe she should have said something else. Maybe she should have retroactively sought this ghost's blessing for absconding with her daughter. Maybe she should have said nothing at all, shut the phone, gone down and apologized.

A chime comes from the navigation booth.

There's a small green light pulsing in the darkness, and after a moment's hesitation and a second chime, Nephele goes to it. She sets Lorelei's phone on the console and strokes her hand over the controls, triggering a soft glow so she can read the labels.

It's a call.

Phones don't work out here, not without a mess of chaotic magic, but expensive, fixed tether points do, and this is the prince's ship. He can afford it. She presses the button to accept the message, and his voice rolls out into the night.

"Corisande."

She forces herself to stand at attention. It's the only thing that makes her feel like the soldier she is, and not the desperate, exhausted wife she's failing at becoming. "My liege."

"Is it done?"

Nephele frowns. "Is what done?" She has had no assignments. She hasn't even spoken to him personally since his pleasure cruise. Reflexively, she reaches for her own phone, but it's still down below, set aside, a useless brick of glass and metal until they return to Volun.

"Your errand." Her prince rarely loses patience, but he sounds…tired. "Are you a widow now, Corisande?"

Her throat tightens. She looks back at the hatch. *Not a widow, no, but maybe no longer wed.* But he can't know that. "I don't understand."

The prince mutters a curse. "It's a secure line, Nephele, don't play coy. Your ship docked over an hour ago. Are you serving her a candlelit dinner first? I never knew you to be inefficient. Or sentimental."

"I'm not *playing coy*," Nephele says, though her heart is sinking low, low, down into her boots.

"Oh, for fuck's sake—why else, with your assistant on the edge of death because of her, would you ask to borrow one of my personal ships to go out into the wastes? A *honeymoon*?"

Yes. Yes, and research, and everything she has already been tasked with, this should not be so confusing. But—

Why else?

Why else would somebody do what she's done? Her mind twists a puzzle piece, slots it into place. Because the wastes are ungoverned. The wastes are lawless. The wastes eat everything up and return nothing.

Because if Lorelei is lost overboard, it will be a tragedy, but not a crime. Not when the Prince of Volun can make it so.

Her hand tightens on the console, tendons standing sharp beneath her skin. Blue light dances across the polished wood of the gunwale, and her wrists ache where the silver begins to react.

"You thought—" she starts, but she sounds like a child, weak, not a soldier. That he would have interpreted her request for a brief holiday as a promise of murder should be an affront, an insult, but of course he could never have expected anything different of her. She is his creature, and he gave her an ultimatum.

She should have questioned when he agreed so readily.

"I thought you would be reasonable," the prince says. Exhaustion shades so quickly into blank chill. "Tell me you are going to be reasonable. Tell me you are going to end our little lingering problem."

End.

End Lorelei.

"I am not the heir to the House of Pharyn," Nephele says. The words echo around the hollow in her chest where her heart has ceased to beat. "If she dies, the House of Pharyn ends. That was not an acceptable outcome."

"You are not the heir, but you will be the executor of the estate. You will be an anchor in the storm to come. You will help me rearrange my city, and allow life to continue." Her prince pauses. "She really has made you foolish, hasn't she?"

"Don't speak of her." Not that way, not any.

"What are you doing, Corisande?"

"I'm solving the puzzle you gave me. I'm saving her life."

"Her life is not worth losing you. I am telling you to come. Come back to me, and to *your* life. I was wrong to order you to do this; I'm fixing it now."

"I can do this. I can fix this. I am *so close*."

But is she? Lorelei's phone glows up at her, accusing. There is still no response. What else hasn't Lorelei told her? And how much does Lorelei hate her, to not trust her, to withhold while playacting pure honesty and affection?

"Time is up, Nephele. There is no harm in admitting failure. But it is embarrassing for you to keep pretending. Playing house? Really?"

"I am not playing."

Her prince sighs. He's ten years younger than she is, but he sounds ageless. It is the throne of Volun sighing, and her head aches, her heart aches. She is being torn in two.

"Come home, General," he says. "War Alchemist. Come home, with or without her, but it is time to move on."

The unreachable tower looms above her. The beam of one of Volun's lighthouses sweeps across it, at this distance only picking out the sharpest of edges, and she steps closer to the railing, desperate to see a figure there. Desperate to see an enemy she can fight. That she can kill.

"Come home," her prince says again, and his voice softens. "You can't save everybody."

And perhaps it's his gentleness that does it.

"No," she says.

And she hangs up.

TWENTY THREE

VENTUALLY, LORELEI STOPS crying.

Without her phone, without outside light, she has no idea how long it's been. She feels hollow. Insubstantial. There's only so much pain one person can take, perhaps, and now that she's reached the limit, her body and mind have realized they must no longer exist. Worn out, wrung out, see-through.

Staggering, she leaves the bed nook and heads for the small bathroom. She is light and fading, but her body still has needs, needs she attends to with automatic gestures, barely thinking. Barely feeling. Perhaps she'll splash some water on her face. Perhaps she'll try to rescue some dignity. Make herself feel less like a scolded child, less like a broken daughter so desperate for comfort that she'd conceal the impossible from the one person who is trying to help her.

Less like the ungrateful wife who wants Nephele to just stop trying.

But then something registers, as she reaches to pull up her clothing.

She's bleeding.

She stares at the flash of red-brown in her undergarments. There isn't much of it. In fact, it looks soaked in. Stained. There's a fresh wet blot in the center, but the rest of it is nearly dry, with an evaporation line around the border.

But it is blood. When she looks in the toilet, the paper is stained.

Oh, she thinks.

What was it Nephele had said? *It's a binary outcome. Either the drinking ends the pregnancy, or it doesn't.*

She supposes they have their answer now. Whatever the text message from her dead mother said, whatever claims of ferocity, blood doesn't lie. Bodies do what bodies will do. Actions have consequences. Lorelei can't just choose to believe otherwise.

The strangest part is…it doesn't hurt.

She's not cramping. There is no deep ache inside of her. Even in hindsight, there was no warning. She's simply bleeding. Slowly, and most of it not even fresh, old blood oxidizing and oozing out of her. Old death, dripping slow. Congealing. Staining everything around her.

Metaphors are a cheap tactic, but she supposes she's earned this.

The short flight of stairs is so narrow and steep that she has to cling to the railing to help herself up. She has no idea what she's going to say, but she can't stay down here, huddled and shivering. She feels *trapped*, but fuck, she's forgotten to wash her hands, she's leaving faint brown marks on the walls. At least she remembered to pull up her clothing.

Maybe she should just lie back down, wait it out. But she won't be able to hide it. Doesn't even want to try. She's already seen how *that* goes.

And maybe Nephele's anger will undo whatever spell

Nephele's disappointment wrought upon her, and maybe *then* she'll fucking feel *something*.

She expects Nephele to be standing at the hatch, waiting in case Lorelei tries to—not escape, but get some fresh air? Break the rules. But she's not there, and Lorelei climbs out into the evening. There's just enough light left to cast a muzzy half-shadow from the tower that stretches above them, closer than she'd seen it from the prince's ship, familiar even from this external angle from her dream.

Her chest squeezes. Nephele knew. Of course she knew. And all Lorelei had to do was surrender, be easy and malleable, and she couldn't even do that right.

She can't stop the small, broken sound that leaks from her throat. She doesn't bother trying.

What is she even doing? She can't do this, can't confess, but she's already crossing the minuscule distance to where Nephele stands in the navigation suite. Her body doesn't even have the decency to stagger. She just walks, the way her uncle trained her to, so properly, and she can't even feel the blood that must be still leaking ever so slowly from between her legs.

"It's happening," Lorelei says, when she reaches the cabin.

Nephele twitches, as if coming back to life. She turns away from the darkened panel.

"What is?"

She sounds as distracted as she looks, glancing towards the city before coming to meet her. She's not hurrying Lorelei back down below. Why not? This close, and in the bright blue cast from the cracks in Nephele's skin, Lorelei can see that the lines around her mouth are starker than usual from how firmly she's holding herself in check.

Nine hells, what if something *else* is wrong? What if she's about to lose her wife and child, all at once?

Lorelei bites down on a shriek and presses the heels of her hands to her eyes.

"Lorelei." Nephele's voice is firmer now, but she hesitates just shy of grabbing Lorelei's hands. She curses, softly; even in the gloom, the blood must be visible. "Lorelei, tell me—"

"The pregnancy."

Because it's not a baby, not yet, never will be, and she suddenly wants to laugh, too, because—because shouldn't she just be grateful? End it all before it gets too painful. End it all before it even feels real.

Her curse is being merciful, for a change.

"I'm bleeding," she says again. "But it doesn't hurt. It doesn't hurt, isn't that wonderful?"

It must be, but when Lorelei looks, Nephele's hands are shaking, and she's staring at her, stricken, hurt, hurting.

"I—you should lie down," Nephele says, and she sounds absolutely lost.

"Why?"

"You should rest. I should—fuck, *fuck*—"

"I did this to myself," Lorelei says, and it sounds so lovely, coming from her mouth. A purgative. Her actions do have consequences, she *can* fuck up her own life, and she didn't know how much she needed to realize that. Her life is still hers. Hers to ruin. She laughs again.

But Nephele, powerful Nephele, has her by the shoulders now, and then by the hips. Her hands skim in, and they are humming with potential. Blue light leaks from her, all over, and her bracelets vibrate.

"Be careful," Lorelei says, startled.

Except she's not careful. She's pressing, and light spills from her, and hovering just beside them, Lorelei can see a throbbing heartbeat.

It beats double-time, the same way it did back home.

"I don't understand," Lorelei says. Her good humor fractures. She sways, and Nephele catches her, hugs her close. "I don't understand, how—it's lying—"

"It's true. It's real, and it's true." Nephele breathes warm against the crown of her head. "We haven't failed yet."

But Lorelei can't breathe. She can only gasp, clutching tight. Because for it not to be over, for it to be fine or in the earliest stages of failure—she can't handle that. She can't carry that weight. A sob breaks from her. "Can you stop it?" she asks, desperately. "Whatever I did, can you protect—I don't—I thought—"

She thought she was okay with the loss, and perhaps she might have been.

But she is not okay with the *losing*.

"Everything is okay," Nephele whispers. "I've done the reading. This happens. This happens, and sometimes it means nothing at all."

"I don't believe you!"

"Trust me, then," Nephele breathes, and all the world is still around them. "Trust me, and let me hold you."

Her head aches. Her eyes burn. She clutches Nephele tight, breathing in the beautiful scent of her, still there, still hers. Nephele cradles her, and Lorelei can feel the shivering of her hands. They shiver together.

And then, in the dark, a sound: Lorelei's phone pinging with a new message.

They move as one, arms twined, hands awkwardly clasped, but it is Lorelei who gets there first, who unlocks the phone and displays the message. The message from her mother.

The message responding to something Nephele sent.

Be strong. Be strong. Be strong.

The tower waits for you.

TWENTY FOUR

TOGETHER THEY STARE at the phone.

"A trap?" Lorelei asks, and Nephele could kiss her, because yes, yes, this sounds exactly like a trap, except—

"Who by?" Nephele casts a wary glance at the bulk of the tower. "Magic? Chaos itself? Neither lends itself to ploys. It's only humans who manage that."

Her hands have not stopped shaking, not since she saw the blood on Lorelei's skin, but this is a challenge. A direct challenge, something Nephele can face head on.

"You want to go," Lorelei says, barely a breath.

"Don't you?"

Lorelei nods.

They would have to nudge the landship even closer to the tower to disembark safely; the more distance they have to travel, the greater chance of something going wrong. When she turns to the navigational controls, Nephele's hands tremble, but the angle of her body hides that from Lorelei.

Pointless, probably; Lorelei already must know how shaken she is tonight, how afraid. If she doesn't, it's only because she, too, is so shattered, so exhausted, so ready to collapse.

And yet with something external to tilt towards, there may be life in them yet.

Steering the landship is not as easy as the tutorial had made it seem. (As her cocksure certainty had made it seem). They lurch in fits and starts, and Nephele almost orders Lorelei belowdecks, but can't get the words out. It might be safer, but she wants her bride close, with her candy-pink hair and her steely determination. If Lorelei is out of sight, Nephele might break.

Lorelei's the first one to spot it.

"We're not getting any closer," she says.

Nephele tears her gaze from the glowing map and looks out over the prow.

"No," she concedes. "We're not."

They are staring up at a different angle of the tower, but one that is no nearer than before. The light remains unchanged. Nephele tries to turn the ship, and it judders, harsh and creaking. An alarm goes off, and Nephele tries to reverse them, hands twitching over the controls. They roll, pitch, and Lorelei has to grab on to the console bank to keep her footing.

"What—"

But Nephele doesn't hear the rest. Everything is azure pain, and she clenches her teeth, fighting to keep herself steady. It crests, needling at the base of her skull, skimming her eye sockets, and then it's gone, leaving behind just the electric-wrong feeling of being twisted about inside her skin. Lorelei is at her side, and in her hands is Nephele's mask. How long has she been out? Blue light dances over the metal; she casts a distinctive glow.

"I'm fine," Nephele rasps.

"Let me," Lorelei says.

She settles the silver across Nephele's brow and cheekbones,

and it is a soft and gentle wave, the lap of an ocean Nephele
has never seen, cooling her blood and settling her nerves.
She has worn limiters like this since she was twelve, and
in the last three decades and change, she has learned
to take them for granted. But here, now, even with the
bracelets already around her wrists, she feels it all anew: the
anchoring, the remove, the whisper of *it'll all be okay.*

She has spent so long knowing that her magic is
something she can control, she's forgotten how to fear it. To
need safety and succor. She'd come close on her wedding
day, but then, she'd had help. An army of researchers.
People who could figure out how to protect her.

Now, she has only Lorelei.

Nephele groans and straightens up; for all her
weakness, she never hit the deck. Beneath her, the ship is
unmoving. When she gains her bearings, she finds they
are a little farther from the tower than they started, but
none the worse for wear, save, perhaps, for her stamina.

Then she looks down at the readouts, and her heart
sinks. "Fuck," she breathes.

"Is the ship okay?" Lorelei asks.

"It is," she says. "But we're not." She jerks her chin
toward the tower. "We'll never get close enough."

Lorelei takes on that stillness she wears when her grief
is sharpest. "What do you mean? We can walk, can't we?
I brought my amulet."

"There's too much warpage." With one finger, she taps
the relevant dial. The indicator spins wildly beneath the
glass. "The way the land folds, it's not evenly distributed,
and there's a limit to what the body and mind can
withstand. What magic can guard against."

Lorelei looks out at the tower. She says nothing.

"I'm sorry," Nephele says.

She turns back to Nephele, and her smile is sweet and
sad, but Rifting take them both, there is that steel inside
of her. "I'm going."

She will not be dissuaded. Nephele can't bring herself to try. But if she steps off this ship, she will be swept far, far away, never to be found again, or perhaps she will simply be crushed, and Nephele will never hold her again.

No.

No, Nephele cannot allow that, either.

(Should she tell Lorelei about the prince's call? About what he expected from her? About how much Nephele is willing to do for her? It is now or never.)

(Never, then.)

So she sets her jaw and holds out a hand. "Then I will go, too. She asked for both of us."

✆

NEPHELE HAS STEPPED through the chaos only twice in her career, and only ever with a strong tether.

This is unlike anything she has ever touched.

One step off of the warded ship, and sunlight breaks over them, harsh and burning. Her stomach lurches. Her body protests, pitching forward, and she clutches hard to Lorelei. "Don't let go," she gasps, even as they fall forward another step—

—cold winter, biting, ice beneath them, Lorelei loses her footing—

—the walls of Lostonten, she has seen these walls, a cry from up above, somebody has seen them appear out of nothing, but this is not where they need to be—

—Nephele vomits into volcanic soil—

—Lorelei's nails drag against her skin as their hold on each other falters in a field of grain—

—one of them is crying, and the world is spinning, spinning, she falls to her knees, she hopes Lorelei falls with her—

—it is too hot, they will boil alive—

—pain—

—"I can't hold on"—

—the mind can only withstand so much—

—abandonment in the wastes without a fixative after surrender is considered a war crime—

—there is a chance of falling into the sea, and does sinking count as directed motion?—

—"Please!"—

—Nephele's hand is empty, no, no, *no,* she let go, when did she—

And then Lorelei's voice, calm and close:

"I can see the tower."

They are in the dry grass wastes outside of Volun. It is dusk. Nephele is on her knees, and her hand is empty, but the world is still, and she is not alone.

Lorelei floats above the cracked earth, eyes open, lips parted. Light shines from her, piercing the gathering dusk. The world snaps and rearranges around them, and Nephele's bones sing with it. Inch by inch, the dirt grows firm, an infinitesimally small reordering that Nephele has spent her entire career attempting to synthesize in such perfect detail.

She stares in awe.

A flicker at the edge of her vision; she turns back, and Lorelei's feet are once more on the ground. Her hand is extended. The light has faded to a soft corona, gleaming in her hair.

This time, when Nephele takes her hand, the world remains, and the tower sits within reach.

ᏇᎱᏋ

BUT THERE IS nobody at the top.

TWENTY FIVE

ORELEI KNOWS THESE stones: blasted, broken, breaking the rules of the world as surely as walking through the maelstrom Rifting had done. The tower is falling apart. Present tense, continuous; it will never fall.

How often has she come here in dreams? It must have been more than the once, because she climbs the final, fragmented steps without hesitation, without issue, despite her exhaustion and the snapback reeling of her senses as the last of the lighthouse glare leaves her mortal again. She knows exactly where to step to preserve her life, and Nephele follows behind her.

And there is nobody else here.

Of course there's nobody; her mother is dead, and the woman in her dreams may never have existed at all. *A trap*, but a trap of nihilism, of pointlessness. What was she expecting to find here? An altar to lay herself across so that whatever curdling of magic lives inside her breast could be excised?

Nephele catches her hand, stops her from taking another aimless step. Lorelei looks back at her for the first time, and she looks so—*tired*.

"Can you get us back?" Nephele asks. "Across the wastes?"

Because they've failed.

They've crossed impossible distances to traverse a few hundred yards. Lorelei glances out past the remaining walls and sees their ship, sitting empty close at hand. Yes, she can get them there, can take them home, but...

But her mother told them to come here. Her mother stilled the chaos in her, brought her safely to Nephele's doorstep, knew before she did that the child she carries is safe. Her mother is real.

"No, there has to be something here," Lorelei says, and bites her lip as she surveys the tower once more. *Something* is here, something she needs to understand. She has to believe that. Maybe it was only the journey, learning what she is capable of? A beacon in the dark, she can stabilize the impossible, and isn't that *enough*?

(Not if Nephele will die from marrying her.)

Nephele shifts beside her, low light catching on her mask. She steps forward, hands raised. She's not wearing her uniform, not out here, but her rank pins still glitter at the collar of her jacket, gleam like the metal of her bracelets, her limiter. Every line of her is tailored, and straining forward with the belief Lorelei has asked of her.

Lorelei holds her breath.

The air begins to hum.

Licorice laces the breeze, and the glow beneath Nephele's face intensifies. Her chin tilts up, back, eyes narrowed, and her hands splay at her sides. Lorelei looks on, seeing Nephele's magic from the outside for the first time since that hateful exhibition so soon after their introduction. It coils in muscles Lorelei has felt beneath dry, cool skin, works along a wicked tongue, and around them, the world begins to kneel to its relentless presence.

Something takes form in the gloaming.

As much as she knows these stones, she has seen this face before, this shape. It is her mother. It is the woman in the tower. It is her own figure in the mirror.

She blinks, and the features shift. An amalgamation, a volatile projection.

And something new. Something she almost recognizes.

Lorelei approaches. Reaches out a hand. The figure doesn't respond, no matter whose face it wears, and is too translucent for any expression to resolve.

"It sees us but doesn't see us," Nephele says from behind her. "Responds to our presence, but is not a presence. Is not a person."

"Just an echo," Lorelei says, heart breaking, as she touches her mother's hand. A blink, and it's her own. Another, and the soldier gazes back at her.

"It was never meant to be a person," the soldier says.

"How did you know it was here?" Nephele asks. "I couldn't sense it at first." Unspoken is *you're not trained for this, you're not made for this, so how?* And perhaps a hint of wounded pride.

"I hoped," Lorelei says. "I was stubborn."

Her mother's face reforms. "Be strong," she says. "You are so strong, dear heart."

"Just tell me what I need to do," Lorelei says, tears welling in her eyes. She has come so far, and all she has to do now is endure, surely. She has grown so good at that, despite herself.

"I can't contain everything inside of me," her own face whispers, voice breaking.

Flicker, flicker, flicker.

"It will never kill you," says her mother. "Not yet, not now, not ever."

"It was never meant to be a person," the soldier echoes. "But it is, it is, it is. Magic made flesh."

And Lorelei begins to understand. Here she is, a girl who should not be who she has become, who has inside of her a lighthouse, a whipcrack chaos, barely leashed. The Rifting, made flesh.

Just a step further than Nephele's latest theory.

"What happens," she asks the flickering mirage, "when I die?"

The image resolves, steadies. The soldier gazes back at her, eyes visible now, sharp beneath the mask. "You go still," the soldier says. "The magic goes still. The land goes still."

It's tempting.

Simple, and tempting. The tower is tall. One misstep, and this is all over: the pain, the loss, even the chaos tearing the world apart. Tearing Nephele apart. She can't contain everything inside of her, and neither can Nephele, and neither can the world.

"Unacceptable," Nephele says, bristling.

And she's right, of course.

Lorelei does not want to die.

"Unacceptable," the memory of a soldier echoes. "The world demands a sacrifice. We must break the world to save it. Unchecked, the emperor will devour everything."

Nephele makes a wounded sound.

Lorelei twists, looking over her shoulder. Nephele stares straight ahead, her jaw quivering, a faint twitch of *no no no*.

A sacrifice—but not Lorelei. If not Lorelei, then who? The seed of a new life inside of her? But Nephele's horror runs deeper than that, something Lorelei can't rightly comprehend.

"The Rifting," Nephele says, voice rough, "was no mistake."

"No mistake. The only way to stop war, to protect everybody. It was never meant to be a person," the soldier says. "A person dies. A person ends. But unchecked, the emperor will devour everything. We must break the world to save it."

Nephele closes her eyes. And then she whispers, "I'll do it."

Lorelei lurches forward, but Nephele is already moving, unclasping her bracelets. They hit the stone, useless, ringing in the dark. "Nephele—"

"It's been done once before," Nephele says. "This spell. I understand, now. The spell's run down, but I can recreate it. I can make it stronger. Stable. And then it will be carved from you, and the world will be safe. You'll be safe."

Lorelei reaches for her, but Nephele catches her by the shoulders, and her arms are longer.

Nephele smiles sadly, thumb stroking along Lorelei's collarbone. "The prince would have had me kill you tonight," she says. "To preserve my life. To preserve his weapon. He doesn't want to believe that I'd choose you over him."

"No," Lorelei pleads.

"But now I don't have to. I can choose both of you. Save your life, and use the Rifting to keep Volun safe."

"No, no, no."

"I've studied for this all my life, Lorelei," Nephele whispers. She leans in, kisses Lorelei's brow. "I have let magic hollow me out and rip me apart. Let me do this. Let me break the world."

Something pulls Lorelei from Nephele's arms, firm and inexorable. She realizes only as it sits her tenderly but unwaveringly on the stone that it is Nephele's power.

And then she watches as Nephele Corisande removes her mask. By the time it hits the stone, the world has already shattered.

TWENTY SIX

NEPHELE'S SCREAMING FILLS Lorelei's lungs, drowning her atop the tower.

Lorelei thrashes on the breaking stone beneath her, while above, Nephele shines brilliant blue, coming apart at the seams. Her clothing is insubstantial against so much power, and fissures of light split across her body, bright and shining, lightning strikes of nervous pathways. Around them, the world buckles, bunching up like fabric seized in clutching hands.

Lorelei forces herself onto her belly, onto hands and knees, and every movement is agony. Physical agony, yes, but beyond that, she is bleeding and yearning and hating. This is not how it was supposed to go. Nephele was never meant to sacrifice herself. This is her wedding night all over again, except she can see Nephele suffer now, can see how she is about to lose her.

Nephele, her wife of circumstance.

Nephele, brilliant and cold and gentle, by turns.

Nephele, who has disobeyed the Prince of Volun for
her.

Lorelei has tried so hard to keep Nephele safe, to push
her away, and failing that, to pretend Nephele doesn't
need protection.

But she does. She is drowning, and Lorelei can't look
away any longer.

So she walks into the storm.

Nephele's sheer power buffets her on all sides, as terrible
as the rifting it feeds into. It clings to her, wrapping tight,
resonating with the double-time beating of her heart. In
the eye of the storm, Nephele's face contorts in pain, but
she does not waver. Not until Lorelei takes another step.
And another.

Lorelei can see Nephele's house. Can see the garden
party, the cathedral, the fertility clinic waiting room.
Every location spins out from beneath Nephele's feet,
every memory, alongside her touch, the warmth of
Nephele's hands on her skin. *Stop*, they beg of her, *rest, let
me do this for you.* But she knows how to do this now, how
to find the steady path amidst the chaos. Lorelei does not
know if she is shining, but she recognizes the undulating,
rippling knots she walks over but cannot see. The body
cannot withstand magic, and neither can the world.
They are all buckling, ripping apart, and this cannot
continue.

She sees herself, briefly, in the dressmaker's mirror,
desperate to flee, desperate to change what cannot be
altered.

And then she sees Nephele's face, overlaid upon hers,
and she finally recognizes the fourth face the echo of the
tower wears.

Their child.

This tower is always falling, always existing; is it such
a stretch, to think it might reach out toward the future as
well as the past?

With a cry, Lorelei throws herself the last few feet to clutch at Nephele's arms, her waist, to press her cheek against her wife's chest. "Please," she whispers. "Please, don't do this alone. Come back to me. I can't—I can't let you sacrifice any more of yourself. I can't *lose you*."

Because a future without Nephele isn't just a terrifying unknown: it's more pain, more loss, and this time, Lorelei refuses to let it crash over her.

She will not let the monster eat her.

She stands up against the force of the storm and kisses Nephele, defiant instead of desperate, demanding instead of begging.

"Please," she whispers against her wife's screaming lips. "Please come back."

Nephele shudders. Her gaze, focused far away, snaps to her, and Lorelei sees it there: the panic and terror inside of her. Her hands grip Lorelei's hips, hard, and don't push her away. She jerks her arm once, twice, and Lorelei looks down to find her pointing to the mask.

Lorelei pulls Nephele with her to the ground, then guides Nephele's hand over the mask. Together, they fit it to her brow. The ragged howl dies in Nephele's throat, and the light dims just enough that they can see around them.

The echo stands nearby, wearing their child's face.

"Do you see it too?" Lorelei asks.

"Yes," Nephele says, voice rasping. Before Lorelei can name what they're seeing, Nephele's hand drops to Lorelei's stomach in confirmation.

"I won't give this up," Lorelei says, throat unexpectedly tight. "Not you. Not the future. I want another way." She tears her gaze away from the echo, looking at Nephele. "Find me another way."

Nephele grimaces. "I am out of ideas."

"You are the greatest alchemist in an age," Lorelei counters. "We have walked through the Rifting. We are in a place of power. *Think*. Go beyond sacrifice. What else is there?"

Nephele opens her mouth to speak, then stops.

She looks down at where she's touching Lorelei.

"Old magic works on a series of complex thaumaturgical resonances," Nephele says. Lorelei can feel her pulse in turn, rabbit fast and pounding. "It can be countered via harmonics. I've done it before, but this—this spell is too wild. Too expansive. It wraps the world. To perceive all of it…"

The child echo cants its head. "It was never meant to be a person," it says. "But it is one."

Nephele's hand on her belly burns.

"You," Lorelei says. "The Rifting was already concentrated in me when you were made. My body, and the potentiate seed from the doctor, and Nephele's magic."

"An imprint and generative force," Nephele says, and there it is, the fierce light in her eyes. Not triumph, but something sweeter still: a theory building, one born out of her training, experience, and power. And born from them, in the purest way. "The embryo encapsulates the Rifting and comes ready-made with a scaffold to amplify my harmonics. I can use it."

"Use?" Lorelei asks, looking at their ghost of a child.

Was it this possibility that was answering Lorelei's texts? That was reaching across a potential future to the moment Lorelei needed her, telling her to be strong, guiding her here?

Does it care about its own existence?

"I think it can withstand the working," Nephele says. Lorelei thinks she might be lying.

"I am so tired," Lorelei says, "of doing things out of obligation."

Leaving her job. Being controlled by her uncle. Married off. Impregnated. Her whole life, for the better part of a year, has been built only on grief, terror, and obedience. And now, to save her wife, to fix the world, she must inflict something upon her future child?

How can she be forced to choose that?

She fists her hands in her hair, closing her eyes, trying

to think. Trying to *see*. If she could change all of this in an
instant, if she could have the life she wanted, what would it
look like? Would she give up Nephele? Would she prefer to
live childless, or try again some other time, with Nephele or
some other partner? Down in the Rifting, she could have
walked through a hundred different lives, or at least the
settings of them.

And yet when she pictures her future, there is Nephele,
come back to her, no longer solely concerned with duty.
And there is a child who looks a lot like the echo across
from them. A child she has ignored the possibility of
whenever possible, leaned into the unreality of, but nine
hells, she hadn't wanted to lose them back on the boat.

She doesn't want to lose them now.

She wants to know them *after* all this. Wants to know
Nephele absent all this chaos. Wants to take her family
through this, to the other side.

A raw pink light washes over her; beside her, Nephele
has painted beautiful colors in the air, weaving in a pattern
Lorelei can't understand. It must show Nephele something
terrible, though; her mouth is set in a worried line.

"What's wrong?" Lorelei asks. "Will it work?"

Nephele hesitates.

"If we do this," she says, finally, "the spell powering the
Rifting will stabilize, and then decay completely."

"Without killing anybody else?"

"Yes, but—"

"Isn't that a good thing?"

"Without the Rifting, Volun will mobilize. Lostonten.
You see that, don't you?" Nephele asks. "So much of
the world for the taking, so fast. Every city state will
scramble for territory. And the cities themselves will be
newly vulnerable, when you can drive a landship right
up to the gates without needing navigational charts and
a programming alchemist, when you can move an army
linearly across the world. There will be war."

The idea makes her blood run cold for just a moment. Then she shakes her head. "Are you so certain that's what will happen?" Lorelei asks, resting her fingers lightly against Nephele's chin, guiding her to look away from the pink glow.

Nephele shudders.

"Are you so certain there is only the capacity for suffering? I have never met my father's family," she says, "because I couldn't afford passage out of Volun. Food is limited because of how much power it takes to keep fields stable, to transport grain back to the cities. The House of Pharyn is a gilded cage. The city of Volun is an iron one. And how much effort have you expended, how much suffering, just to keep us fed? How much has the Rifting already broken you?"

"Volun needs me."

"*I* need you," Lorelei says. "And you have given Volun enough. Please. Please, stay with me. Be my wife, Nephele."

She fully expects rejection. This last step, a step too far. Nephele has lived so many decades without her, bound to a specific idea of herself. Of goodness.

But Nephele must feel it too, the electric bond between them, because after a moment, she nods. "Very well."

If only Lorelei couldn't see the shadow behind her eyes. If only Lorelei didn't know her so well.

"What aren't you telling me?" she asks, voice as soft and vulnerable as she can make it.

Nephele's stoicism falters.

"When the Rifting goes," Nephele says, "It may take my power with it. Like the vacuum formed when something immeasurably heavy is dropped into water. And without it…"

Nephele's shoulders begin to quiver, and Lorelei reaches out. Draws her close, holds her tight.

"What will I be?" Nephele asks, and her voice is breaking. "If I cannot protect Volun, if I cannot protect you, what am I?"

"Alive," Lorelei answers.

She laces their fingers together. Nephele still shakes, but the trembling slows, and slows, until she grows still and calm at last.

"Alive," Nephele agrees, quietly. "Alive, and with you. Yes."

To make this choice will change the world.

To make this choice will be the most selfish thing Lorelei might ever do.

"Should we name them?" Lorelei asks, looking over at the echo.

"Something to make it real," Nephele agrees. "What was your mother's name?"

"Reyni," says Lorelei, and her smile goes beyond the curve of her lips, down into her heart, her bones. *Reyni.* The name feels right. Feels perfect.

"I'm so happy to meet you, Reyni," she says.

Nephele kisses Lorelei's brow, then goes to work.

This time, the world does not shatter.

It's a gentle slide, a touch but not a touch, that skims her skin and slides just beneath it. It's the whisper of a sensation, the promise of a caress. Nephele's power wraps around her, flows through her veins, nests in her belly. Lorelei leans into it, holds on through the storm that kicks up in the center of her, the reorganization and alchemical coalescing of their hearts.

And all of it feels like home.

TWENTY SEVEN

HEY WAKE TO grey predawn light atop an old stone tower, its blocks fitting neatly together except for where the mortar has crumbled with time. There is a ship, sitting just below them. Their ship. When they make their way to it, the ground is steady beneath their feet. Inside, the sheets are still rumpled from where Lorelei curled up in them. There is still dried blood on the stair hallway. Nephele's codes light up the navigation console.

An error message blinks up at them, crimson and shining: **PATHING UNRECOGNIZABLE. CHECK CALIBRATION.**

Nephele looks out over the bow, back toward Volun. It sits where it always has, the land between her and it traversable, if only one knows how. The ship is warded. But the maps are all wrong, and her only choice, as she shifts the ship into manual control, is to follow the lighthouse, shining out from the eastern wall, back across the plains.

And is it any wonder, then, that the world remains steady, and the sun continues to rise?

ଔଔ ଔଔ ଔଔ

ACKNOWLEDGMENTS

THIS BOOK OWES its existence to the confluence of three things.

First: the video game *Dishonored* and, specifically, my fic-writing obsession with one Callista Curnow. She's a minor character whose entire family has died, save for her and her uncle. (Sound familiar?) Her curse is never examined at any length in game, but that didn't stop me from writing fic about her arranged marriage with another character specifically to preserve her fortune, and how they caught feelings. *Scenes From A Marriage* is, for the record, *extremely* different from this book, and is more about family drama, alcoholism, miscommunications, and a very pissed off ocelot. But it was on my mind when…

Next: the pandemic happened, and early on, Jo Walton and Maya Chhabra put together *The New Decameron*, a fundraising anthology of short stories and excerpts of whatever tales contributors wanted to submit. I am decidedly *not* a short story writer, and I didn't have any work I could excerpt…

...except for an opening scene very similar to the first chapter of this book. Would they like me to expand it into something a bit longer? Oh yes! And thus was born "In This, At Least, We Are Alike," which was an earlier form of chapters one, six, and seven.

And last: dave ring asked for a novella. I sent in some ideas, including this one; it was "In This, At Least, We Are Alike" that won him over. The result is this book: achingly sad, probably too honest on a few points of my own fertility struggles and grief, and a huge gamble in terms of audience.

I hope you have enjoyed this book. I hope it's made you swoon, or sigh, or tear up. Lorelei and Nephele are so unlikely and so dear to my heart, and it has been an honor to share their story with you.

Finally, a thank you to my agent, Caitlin McDonald, my first readers, Alex and Integra, and my family. We made it through another one. :)

ABOUT THE AUTHOR

Caitlin Starling is the bestselling and award-winning author of *Last to Leave the Room*, *The Death of Jane Lawrence*, and *The Luminous Dead*. She writes genre-hopping horror and speculative fiction, and has been paid to invent body parts. You can find links to her work and social media at www.caitlinstarling.com.

OTHER NEON HEMLOCK TITLES BY CAITLIN STARLING

Yellow Jessamine (2020)

ABOUT THE PRESS

Neon Hemlock is a Washington, DC-based small press publishing speculative fiction, rad zines, and queer chapbooks. Publishers Weekly once called us "the apex of queer speculative fiction publishing" and we're still beaming. Learn more about us at neonhemlock.com and on social medias at @neonhemlock.